SUMMER OF '79

Collins & Halsey Publishers / November 2017

ISBN: 978–0-998983011

Cover Design: *www.vividcovers.com*

Interior Design & Formatting: Christine Borgford of Type A Formatting / *www.typeaformatting.com*

Editing: Lauren I. Ruiz of Pure Text / *www.pure-text.net*

ALSO BY
DARREN SAPP

Fire on the Flight Deck
The Fisher Boy
Aaron Bank and the Early Days of US Army Special Forces
Special Force: A World War II Commando Novel

Discover more at *www.darrensapp.com*
and join the mailing list.

SUMMER OF '79

DARREN SAPP

Dedicated to Todd Francoise, Scott Johnson, Grant Qualls, Greg Qualls, Frank Sapp, Thad Thrash, Matt Welch, Johnny Woodall, Carl Jones, Brad Biggar, and Bobby Jankowski.

They were the greatest bunch of guys to grow up with. We had thousands of hours of hide-and-seek, board games, bowling, swimming, Fort Zot, and of course, hanging out in those woods.

You never forget the friends you grew up with.

—Unknown

CHAPTER 1

"HUGE! MASSIVE! THE biggest we've ever done," Kevin told his best friend Larry Woodard.

They made their final bus trip home from W. A. Thompson Junior High School on the last day of their seventh-grade year. They sat in the middle of the bus on the hump. Ninth graders were privileged with the back seats.

Two of those ninth graders engaged in a pencil fight—one held his pencil horizontally and the other tried to snap it in half with his pencil. The back end of the bus was always more noisy and rowdy.

A few students turned toward Kevin at his emphatic statements.

Larry elbowed him. "Shush. Remember, this is a secret."

"Yeah, yeah, I get it." Kevin lowered his head and whispered, "I'm just sayin' this is gonna be the most massive fort we've ever built. Nothin' like last summer. This thing's gonna be huge. I've been drawin' it out." He opened his Trapper Keeper to reveal a drawing.

Larry slapped the top of the binder closed. "Not here."

Screeeeeech!

The bus stopped near an aging oak tree that cast a shadow over the street.

Larry had darted toward the front before the wheels came to rest.

Kevin stood and stepped into the aisle as a larger teen barreled by, forcing him back down into his seat.

Larry waited by the curb for Kevin to step off, and they made the trek up a hilly street for their homes—one next to the other. They lived on Ridgeview Lane in a tract-home community where every street seemed to have the name "ridge" in it, like Ridgeway, Pine Ridge, or Ridgecrest.

"I guess Slade was 'sick' again today," Larry said with air quotes.

Kevin chuckled. "Yeah, he told me he was skippin'. He started summer vacation a couple of weeks ago if you know what I mean. I don't know how he gets away with it."

"Boo!"

Kevin and Larry each took a step back, startled.

Slade Littlejohn laughed after jumping out from behind the red-tip photinia that consumed the corner of his home's side lawn at the top of the hill. He wore cut-off Wranglers but no shirt or shoes. Unlike his friends, his athletic build had already taken form.

He flexed his muscles in mockery. "How was school today, suckers?"

"How do you get away with it?" Kevin asked with one eye squinted as he faced the sun.

"Ain't that funny? Y'all are dumb enough to go to school on the last day, and I'm smart enough to get out of it. I just told my mom the last day was optional if we have all our work turned in and tests done."

"Optional?" Larry said with a raised eyebrow.

Slade smirked. "I might have made that up. When are we gettin' started on the fort?"

"Let's go tonight," Kevin said.

"Can't," Larry said. "Got a game."

Slade began to walk off. "Yep. I've got baseball too. I'm pitchin'. We'll go in the mornin'. Later, gator. I mean, suckers." He spit toward the bushes for no particular reason.

"After while, crocodile," Larry said.

They slow-walked the length of nine more homes to their houses. The summer heat was almost bearable when talking about nothing with your best friend. It could have been worse. It could have been one of those triple-digit days, but the after-school temperature peaked at ninety-two that day.

"Wanna come to my game tonight?" Larry asked.

Kevin shrugged. "I'll ask my mom. But, she's makin' Sloppy Joes tonight. My favorite. Don't want to miss that." He chuckled.

"Luckeeey! I love those. We just get leftovers on game nights. Pork chops and applesauce," he said in his best Peter Brady voice. "It's the late game, though. Be outside at six thirty."

"K. Later." Kevin broke off from Larry and walked across the St. Augustine lawn toward his 3–2-2 brick-veneer home. Wax leaf ligustrum shrubs lined the house, but the heat had reduced his mother's marigolds to curled brown residue. The basketball net was frayed from birds picking away pieces for their nests.

Larry headed toward a home that was almost identical except for some subtle differences in trim, paint, and shrubbery.

Their homes, their neighborhood, and their town were nothing exceptional. Some might have described it all as boring. The youth made that claim as well, but the older folks liked it boring. Quiet. Peaceful. Mead Creek residents liked to say their town was halfway between somewhere and nowhere.

MEAD CREEK, TEXAS, was known for two things: a Civil War battle—a skirmish, really—where the Confederates won a decisive victory, and the unsolved triple murder of the Claymore family. Locals boasted about the former but shunned the latter. The 1912 murder left a stain on the town that had lasted sixty-seven years. Various law enforcement agencies chased multiple leads for years. An English detective that had once worked the Jack the Ripper case even sailed over to lend his expertise. As the First World War ramped up, interest in the case dwindled for most aside from the occasional amateur sleuths, who would roll into town for a few days of investigation.

Most wanted to move on. As the summer of 1979 began, the modern decade of the eighties loomed. Kids would escape the heat in the swimming pool as their parents strategically placed box fans throughout the house. Boys would kick up dirt on the baseball field, and girls would giggle through the night at slumber parties. Most families had vacation plans or might take a day trip to Six Flags Over Texas amusement park.

Kevin Bishop and friends had talked for weeks about summer plans. They'd travel daily to the nearby woods for a special building project that they would continue that summer, and only their small circle knew of its whereabouts.

That was the plan for them and the folks in Mead Creek. Their plans would change.

CHAPTER 2

"SAFE!" KEVIN DECLARED as he stepped on a crushed
Coca-Cola paper cup.

"Bull crud! I pegged you before you stepped on
home," Damon "Rut" Rutledge said defiantly.

The stakes weren't quite as high as they were for the baseball
games occurring on the fields to each side of them. This was a
game of cup ball played under three towering silver maples. No
bats or gloves were needed. The "ball" was one crumpled cup
stuffed inside another cup that was then crumpled. Other cups
or trash served as the bases with bare, open hands for bats and
gloves. Three could play, but the more, the better. It passed the
time for those like Kevin, who didn't play baseball, or Rut, who
had finished his game.

Rut's dad, also his coach, wanted to watch the next game and
scout their next opponent's best players. Most dads watched and
second-guessed the coaches as the moms cheered their children's
success or error.

Larry played on one field and Slade on another. When the
official games ended, Kevin watched a few innings of their cup
ball match before joining in on the action. He wasn't much of an

athlete and remained a child at heart although six months into his thirteenth year—blond hair turning brown. He paid less attention to his appearance and focused on other pursuits, such as building a fort.

Rut lived one street over from them and always wanted to hang out with the trio of Kevin, Larry, and Slade. They wouldn't go out of their way to let him know their plans, but if he happened to find them, they welcomed him. A year younger and much smaller, Rut had a Napoleonic complex. No one considered him a tough guy, and he avoided confrontation. However, he'd challenge anyone, anytime, anywhere to a fight over insults to his stature.

The previous fall, he had excelled as his pee wee football team's starting running back. His coach, inadvertently, said, "Look at that Rut go." The coach meant no harm and called him Rut, in short, for his last name: Rutledge. His teammates thought the coach called him "runt" in reference to his short stature. One teammate decided that would be a great nickname until Damon drove his helmet into his midsection. Damon didn't care for being called Rut but learned early that the more one fights a nickname, the more it will stick. The teammates settled on Rut and Damon accepted.

After Rut's emphatic statement that he had pegged Kevin with the cup ball before he stepped on home, Kevin looked to Rut's teammate for umpiring.

The teammate offered a shrug and upturned hands.

"Whatever. Y'all win. I'm tired of playin'," Kevin said. He rubbed the wax from the paper cup off on his shorts.

That's how cup ball went.

Kevin and Rut walked toward Larry's game. "Your sister, Wendy, here?" Kevin asked.

"Nope. Why?" Rut asked, almost annoyed.

"Just wonderin' . . . if your whole family comes to games."

"Oh. Usually, but they drove separate and left," Rut said. "What are y'all doin' tomorrow?"

Kevin looked to the side. "Don't know."

"Don't know? The first day of summer vacation and you don't know? We can sleep in, go bowlin', swim, play Monopoly, go to the dollar movie, hang out at the arcade, do anythin' we want."

Kevin shrugged.

"Well. Call me if y'all do somethin'."

"I don't know. You have a bunch of nines in your number. Lot of work to dial all that. Takes a long time," Kevin said with a smile.

"Ha, ha," Rut said. He walked up the bleachers and sat by his father.

Kevin walked past Larry's dugout and leaned on the four-foot fence next to three men. One of them stuffed a wad of Red Man chewing tobacco between his cheek and gums.

The sun had disappeared over the horizon, dropping the temperature to a tolerable level. The buzzing of the baseball field lighting sounded off, and June bugs began to gather. Singing cicadas made their presence known.

Kevin endured several innings as the game wound down. He didn't care about the outcome. The players lined up and met at midfield, slapping hands, and saying, "Good game," to one another.

Kevin met Larry walking out of the dugout. "Man, did you see that hit I got? Pegged the outfield fence."

"Uh, yeah. That was a good one," Kevin lied.

The pair noticed Slade by the next field, mimicking a catch and throw he'd likely done in the game.

Several parents, players, and younger siblings climbed into cars as the parking lot emptied and the evening grew darker.

The fathers of Slade and Rut plus two more dads gathered around a 1974 green Chevrolet pickup. Slade's dad had stopped at Piggly Wiggly on the way to the ballpark and iced down a case of Old Milwaukee. A few other dads gathered in other locations around the ballpark's four fields. For the dads, the first half of the evening involved baseball and the second half involved game recaps and the occasional dirty joke over a cold beer.

Some boys moved their cup ball game to one of the now empty fields.

Kevin, Slade, and Larry sat on swings but only swung enough to make grooves in the dirt with their feet.

"Now, where again are we supposed to get enough wood to build a fort?" Slade asked Kevin.

"Told ya. When we were out there a few weeks ago, there was this collapsed shed. We can use that for the walls. But we'll need more stuff. We can get it off that scrap pile at Pollard's Lumber. We'll just grab a few pieces each day and carry it out there."

"Yeah, man. We've got this all figured out. We can take all the tools on the first couple of trips and then hide them so we don't have to carry them back and forth each time," Larry said. "It's the perfect spot. Nobody goes out there. Nobody will find it."

"Who else we gonna invite?" Slade asked.

Kevin shrugged. "Just us for now. Maybe after it's built, we recruit a couple more guys. Won't be fun if we have too many."

"Might be easier to use the main road to get there. Avoid all the dips and bumps on that dirt road," Larry said.

Slade, indignant. "What? No way. We're goin' down Devil's Backbone. The other way is like an extra two miles. You ain't chicken, are ya?"

Larry, equally indignant. "No. I just think—"

"Why are y'all talkin' about Devil's Backbone?" Rut said, walking up behind them.

The three looked at one another, unsure of their next move.

"Just tell him. He's gonna find out anyway," Slade said.

Larry nodded.

Kevin nodded as well. "All right. We're gonna build a massive fort out by Meyer's Pond."

"Oh, cool!" Rut said.

"But don't tell anybody. It's a secret. We don't want a bunch of guys findin' out. We're gettin' started first thing in the mornin' and we're using Devil's Backbone to get there."

Rut, excited at first, began to frown. "Devil's Backbone?"

CHAPTER 3

BOUT THE TIME Mead Creek kids began journeying around town on their bicycles, some older kid would tell them about the Devil's Backbone challenge. The dare had to be done alone, and preferably at dusk. Only the bravest did it after dark.

The old lane once connected a few farms to town but was no longer a usable road for vehicles. Overgrown with brush, only off-road bicycles navigated its bumps and craters. The only thing of note along the route was the old Claymore estate and family cemetery.

The telling of the legend always started the same. Near the turn of the century, the whole Claymore family was murdered, and the old mansion remained abandoned. Or was it? To deepen the fear factor, an experienced storyteller would say that if you rode past it at the time of day the murder happened, you'd hear the screams of the victims. The murders were so gruesome that it seemed no ordinary man could have done it, and the murderer still roamed the woods near the house.

Slade had taken the dare, not once, but twice. Kevin and Larry, however, avoided the rite of passage and took the hit to their pride. They'd ridden down a handful of times, but always in a group.

—◦●◦—

THE CREW AGREED on a 10:00 AM meet-up in front of Rut's house, since it was on the way. Kevin, Larry, and Slade rode up to find Rut and his older sister, Wendy, sitting on their bikes in the driveway.

Larry rode the latest Mongoose model—a recent birthday gift from his grandparents. The rest settled for bikes with no significant branding or that were put together with spare parts. Other than Wendy's five-speed Schwinn, they were designed for off-road use.

Wendy had recently turned fourteen, was slightly older than the four boys, and had finished her eighth-grade year. Her clothing style matched the boys' although she was a thin, yet developing girl, with long brown hair pulled back in a tight ponytail.

Slade and Larry wore Wrangler cutoffs and tank tops while the rest sported their school's athletic shorts and T-shirts. All had socks with various-colored stripes pulled over the calf and each wore tennis shoes.

"Where y'all goin'?" she asked.

"Nowhere. Just ridin' around," Slade answered.

Wendy smirked. "Really? Not goin' bowlin'?"

"Yeah. Probably bowlin'," Larry answered.

"Bull. Rut already told me about the fort." Wendy popped up her kickstand.

Larry threw up his arms. "Rut!"

"I had to," Rut said. "She made me. She was fixin' to call my mom. She's in charge while my parents are at work, and she asked where I was goin'."

"So, you lie, idiot," Slade said.

Rut crossed his arms. "Nope. I never lie. Plus, I can't go unless she comes."

"Whatever," Slade said. "She'll get tired of it after one day. Just please don't tell anyone."

"Humph. I won't tell anyone about your dumb fort," Wendy said with a long eye roll.

Slade shook his head at Kevin. "We're like the Little Rascals and she's Darla."

———— • ● • ————

JUST UNDER A quarter mile from their neighborhood, they entered Mead Creek's downtown. The last day of school had been a Tuesday, so that Wednesday morning saw the normal hustle and bustle of town as folks ran errands and businesses welcomed customers.

Slade popped a wheelie and held it for twenty feet.

Rut tried the same but failed.

They rode past the stone courthouse built in 1928, which housed all things government related. A fire took the original courthouse where more than one murderer and horse thief had been convicted and hanged.

The town square housed a veterans monument in the center surrounded by a lawn and benches. The designer of the granite monument wanted riders of horses and buggies to take notice and pay homage as they made their way through the center of town. The top six names belonged to Confederate soldiers, two of whom were brothers. A local craftsman added the name of one World War I veteran, but Mead Creek gave nine sons to World War II. Only six years previous, the names of two draftees that had lost their lives in Vietnam were added.

A local city councilman had once suggested moving the monument to aid traffic flow. He was soundly defeated in the next election. The kids had passed the monument many times but never took the time for reading and remembrance.

The First Baptist Church steeple poked above the downtown buildings, but drivers headed toward Mead Creek on State Highway 370 would first notice the water tower. HOME OF THE MEAD CREEK WILDCATS was stenciled across each side, recognizing the local high school team.

Nineteenth-century buildings were connected to more recent construction. The oldest building, built in 1876, housed a gift and flower shop, though its façade was painted for a more modern look.

Avoiding traffic, the teens moved onto the sidewalk, nearing Pollard's Hardware, a fixture on the square that had begun in the previous century as Pollard's General Store.

The elderly but agile Ephraim Pollard stepped out of his business and onto the sidewalk.

Slade, in the lead, widened his eyes and braked hard. The rest followed suit as Kevin's bike ran into Slade's.

Pollard turned and ripped off his fedora. "You kids ain't supposed to be ridin' on the sidewalk. Now get off." One eye squinted a little harder than the other, and his unshaven face made for a harsh scowl.

The kids stared back in fear.

Three agonizing seconds later, Wendy answered for the group, "Yes, sir."

Pollard smoothed his sparse white hairs over his bald spot and returned his hat.

They walked their bikes off the sidewalk and resumed their trek down the street.

"Man, that was a close one," Kevin said.

Slade looked over his shoulder at the hardware store. "Who cares about that old dude?"

Larry nodded. "I know, right? He's so dang mean. Don't know what anyone ever did to him."

"Hey, I want a Coke. Let's go to Dairy Queen," Rut said.

"Yeah, I gotta go to the bathroom anyway," Kevin said.

Slade shook his head. "Man, we just left home. Besides, you can take a leak in the woods."

Wendy cleared her throat. "Maybe others need to go."

Slade looked at her and smiled. "Oh, yeah. Guess you can't take a leak in the woods."

"I could, but I don't want to," she answered.

"C'mon. Just for a minute," Rut said, steering his bike into the Dairy Queen parking lot.

The rest followed and laid their bikes down. Wendy used her kickstand.

A green Caprice waiting behind another car inched forward in the drive-thru as they left the outside heat.

An uninspired middle-aged woman took Rut's order as Larry and Slade took turns at the water fountain.

Larry elbowed Slade and nodded toward a booth across the restaurant.

Two girls sipped their drinks and giggled. One of them waved. "Hey, Slade."

Slade gave a head lift, acknowledging their greeting but playing it cool. He had recently dumped his girlfriend of two months seeking his freedom for the summer break.

Kevin emerged from the bathroom to the sound of cards slapping on a nearby table.

The DQ Bunch, as they were known, consisted of several elderly men that assembled at the same round table every day. Some came for morning coffee and left, but a few stayed for cards until lunchtime or later for an afternoon session. The restaurant's owner had placed a name plate at their table with INFORMATION DESK engraved.

Locals jokingly entrusted these elderly men for all Mead Creek history, gossip, current affairs, and sports commentary. They relished the opportunity to put their cards down and wow listeners with their deep knowledge.

Unlike the adolescents, the old men wore button-down shirts and long pants, except for one, who wore overalls with a ball cap. "That son of a gun is running this country into the ground," one said.

"You think ole Jerry Ford would be doing any better?" another countered.

The cacophony of ramblings confused Kevin as one old man interrupted another.

The DQ Bunch would notoriously switch from politics to sports to the price of eggs with rapid precision. The group had three veterans of World War I although one always referred to that conflict as The Great War. If his health allowed, ninety-nine-year-old Jacob Carver was brought to DQ once or twice per week by his son. The oldest of the bunch had served in the Spanish-American War, but not with Teddy Roosevelt's Rough Riders as he'd always clarify.

Kevin leaned in to hear what Carver said, as his feeble voice was drowned out by others.

"I remember a time when—"

"Kevin! C'mon!" Larry said, holding the door.

The others were mounting their bikes.

Kevin looked up, almost startled. He walked to the door as one ear focused on the DQ Bunch.

The green Caprice moved up to the drive-thru window.

Construction workers hammered and drilled next to Dairy Queen.

"What's that?" Rut said. "Looks like they're buildin' the Alamo."

"Taco Bell, coming soon," Larry read on a sign.

Rut's front tire waddled as he looked to the side. "Cool! We need more Mexican restaurants."

They looked both ways before crossing State Highway 370 at the edge of downtown. They saw no cars, and on some days one might not see a car pass by the town for a half-hour. Just miles of highway that glistened in the morning sun.

Pollard's Lumber, owned by the same family that ran the hardware store, was the only business on the other side of the highway. A few cars sat in the parking lot, and a forklift operator moved a pallet through a gated area of fencing.

Kevin stopped them once they made their way behind the lumber yard. "See. Check out all that scrap. We can use it for the fort."

"Will they let us have it?" Larry asked.

"We don't want to ask. They might tell us 'no,'" Slade said. "It's better to ask forgiveness than permission. One of my rules. If we get caught, we'll just say we thought it was trash."

Kevin swatted his hand. "We can talk about it later. Today's more of a scoutin' mission. We need to figure out the best spot and make plans."

Seventy yards down, they stopped at the entrance to Devil's Backbone.

CHAPTER 4

THEY COULD HAVE simply kept on riding into Devil's Backbone. However, Slade stopped the group to ponder its eerie entrance.

There wasn't any gate or barrier. Remnants of an old gas station barely stood about forty yards away. The tall gas pump was long gone and the boards covering the windows barely clung to the structure. Legend suggested that Bonnie and Clyde had once fueled their Ford V8 at the station in between robberies. Long ago, someone heading down Devil's Backbone may have found the store a comfort before they traveled the dirt road. Now, what remained of the building only reminded the teens that it was their last glimpse of civilization before heading into the abyss.

Slade looked at Rut and Wendy. "Y'all ever been back here?" he said, with an evil grin.

"Nope!" Wendy answered, defiantly. "Ain't no big deal." She straddled her bike, one foot on a pedal, and folded her arms.

Rut simply shook his head.

Slade proceeded to share his version of the Devil's Backbone legend but offered his own twist. "I heard about ten years ago that a kid took the dare and hasn't been seen since."

"That's bull crud!" Rut said.

Larry shook his head. "Nuh-uh. I heard it too."

"They're just tryin' to scare you," Wendy said. "Don't listen to 'em."

"Well, anybody gonna take the dare? Gotta ride all the way past the Claymore mansion to the cemetery, touch the gate, and come back."

"Or what?" Wendy asked.

Slade looked to the side. "Or you're chicken. But, if you survive it, then you did it."

Wendy scoffed. "That's so stupid. Let's just go."

"Yeah, we don't have time for that anyway," Kevin said.

Slade shrugged. "All right. Just tryin' to keep y'all from bein' chickens." He led the group and pedaled down the twelve-foot-wide lane, the others close behind.

They had missed the sign hidden behind years of overgrown brush that read, NO TRESPASSING. PRIVATE ROAD. Only the "NO" part of the top left could be read by those paying attention.

The group followed Slade single file to take advantage of his navigation of each bump, crevice, and puddle left by the most recent rain. Kevin brought up the rear. It didn't take long for them to reach stretches where trees formed an arch over the road and blanked out much of the sun. Their entire trip measured just under one mile from the highway to Meyer's Pond, where they had planned to build the fort.

Kevin spotted remnants of a barbed wire fence attached to leaning posts that ran parallel to the lane. He pondered the farmer who might have built it. What once kept livestock fenced in was now holding brush back from overtaking the road.

They crossed a rickety bridge that likely hadn't seen any maintenance since its initial construction. The dry creek bed below had likely once forked from the main creek.

"Stay to the right!" Slade barked, warning them to avoid a gaping hole from three missing boards on the left that exposed the creek below them.

Pop! Pop! Pop!

The wooden bridge reflected each bicycle and rider's weight as they coasted across.

The Claymore estate sat halfway down Devil's Backbone at a bend. Some called it a mansion while others considered it a large home. To Mead Creek teenagers and children, it was "the mansion." Slightly beyond the house, the family cemetery had three gravestones, leaning in one direction or another. Many kids taking the dare never made it to touch the cemetery gate, finding the house far too terrifying to pass by.

— •◉• —

SLADE RODE BY the house, offered it a cordial glance, and kept riding.

Directly behind him, Larry gave it a few glances, raised up on his bike, and sped up.

Next, Wendy, then Rut, slowed their pedaling and took in the structure, looking up and down.

Kevin, in the rear, wanted to speed up but was forced to wait on the others. He'd seen the house several times but never really studied it.

The dark gray exterior may have been original paint or simply the lack of paint on aged wood. All the doors and windows remained intact and closed. One shutter was askew and looked as if it could fall at any moment. Four A-framed pieces sat over second-floor windows. In the center, a cone-shaped structure protruded from the roof to make for a third floor. Kevin thought it might serve as a watchtower.

Unlike his father's immaculately cared-for lawn, the Claymore lawn had multiple varieties of weeds and grasses. Sand burrs with stickers and dandelions pointed in every direction. The stone walkway leading from the road to the house was broken in several places. Trees towered over the home, with one huge branch resting on the roof. A porch wrapped around the home, and one side sagged with several rails missing.

Two outbuildings matched the look of the home. Kevin assumed one might be used for storage and the other as a garage.

As Rut and Wendy sped to catch the now far-ahead Slade, Kevin took one last look at the house. His eyes wandered to the corner second-floor window.

A face stared back.

Kevin immediately averted his eyes, hoping it had not really happened. He looked back to see the face again. A strong chill ran down his back. He squeezed his pelvic muscles to prevent urine from trickling out. He wanted to cry out to his friends. They had turned at a bend by the cemetery and he could barely see them. He needed their help. He opened his mouth but no sounds emerged.

The cemetery to his left seemed to cry out. To reach out and grab him. To keep him at the estate.

He pedaled harder, finally catching up to them. Should I tell them? he thought. He chose silence. They wouldn't believe he'd just seen a ghost.

• ● •

SLADE SLAMMED ON his brakes with a dramatic slide into a ninety-degree turn. He looked back for his friends.

Larry and Rut mimicked the slide with less flair.

Wendy simply stopped. She reached down, pulled up a handful

of dandelion-like weeds, and blew the white seed heads off.

Kevin rolled to a slow stop.

They reached Meyer's Pond at an open area where the lane narrowed. The pond had been fished out years before, and few signs of aquatic life existed. The murky water had a dark green color with a visibility of less than an inch. Reeds filled one end of the pond. Insects darted across the water's surface.

The midday sun beat down on their necks. An ant mound the diameter of a tire rose above the surrounding weeds. Red ants scurried about with some unknown intention.

Slade hopped off his bike, picked up a rock, and attempted a throw from one side to the other. He tossed with full might, but the rock barely made it halfway.

Wendy looked over at Kevin. "Somethin' wrong? You look funny."

Kevin turned to her, silent for two seconds. "What? No. I'm fine."

"So, where we buildin' this thing?" Rut asked.

Kevin pointed. "That way. Follow me."

Kevin pedaled his bike over deep grass toward a clump of trees. He passed between two of them as the others followed. A trail meandered through more trees and brush for forty yards to another open area.

Water flowed down a creek with a clear view to the bottom, unlike the water of the lifeless pond. Large, smooth rocks diverted the water on one side.

Kevin sat his bike down and moved to the flat area next to the creek. "This is the spot. It's perfect." He pointed and directed with his hands. "We can put the door right here and have a window on this side. And we have water right here. We can even catch craw-dads and cook 'em. We got everythin' we need."

"What's the point?" Wendy asked.

"The point of what?" Slade asked back.

"The point of havin' a fort. Are you defendin' somethin'? Is there some army gonna attack you? Cranville Hornets?" She referred to a neighboring town's middle school.

Slade, indignant. "What? No. Just a fort. To hang out. Like a clubhouse."

"Yeah. Just a place for us. So, you can't tell anyone," Larry said.

"Yeah, can't tell no one," Rut needlessly chimed in.

Kevin waved his arm. "C'mon. Let's get the stuff we need."

Leaving their bikes, they were led by Kevin through heavy brush, including several thorn bushes. They pressed on, using their shoes to stomp down the long, thorny annoyances, but each of them gained a few scratches.

Wendy slapped her neck to extinguish a bug.

Forty feet from the creek bed, Kevin stopped. "Here it is," he proclaimed.

The pile may have been an outbuilding many decades ago. A wall lay atop another with other remnants nearby.

Kevin grabbed one end and pulled, moving the top piece less than a foot. "C'mon, help me."

Larry and Slade grabbed on but failed to move it. One pushed as another worked against him.

"Hey, Moe, Larry, and Curly. You need to all lift and pull the same way," Wendy said.

They obeyed and slid the top piece completely off the pile to reveal another. Some of the wood had rotted from termites as well as decades. Piece by piece, they dragged the materials to the fort site and leaned them on trees.

The tall and full trees protected them from the sun, but the lack of any breeze made for unbearable working conditions. They each broke into a sweat.

Kevin used his heel to mark the outline for the structure. "If we cut those long pieces off, we can use the extra for the roof."

"We should dig out trenches and set the walls in 'em. That way the walls will be more sturdy," Larry said.

The others looked at him with no objection.

"Sounds good," Slade said. "Let's use those metal pieces."

The nearby pile had several metal bars with sharp angles. They each began carving a trench along Kevin's heel marks. The clay soil required great effort.

After four minutes of toil, Larry said, "Maybe we don't need trenches."

"Yes, we do," Slade said. "Just keep at it. It'll get easier once we break the hard stuff."

Wendy stabbed at her trench, hoping to gain some advantage. *Clank!*

Wendy cocked her head. She stabbed again. *Clank!*

"I think I hit somethin'."

"Probably a rock," Kevin suggested.

She worked her metal bar under the object and pried. A round metal piece emerged. "This ain't no rock."

The others stopped their digging and surveyed the find.

"Wonder what that is," Rut said.

All hands began working the dirt around the object, abandoning Kevin's carefully laid-out markings.

"There's more!" Rut declared. "It's long."

They dropped to their knees and used their fingers and hands.

"Part of it's wood. Maybe it's just some kind of tool," Slade said.

Kevin opened his mouth. "It's a gun! It's a gun."

"Whoa!" Rut said.

"It's a shotgun!" Slade said. "Careful pullin' it up. The wood part is barely hangin' on."

Slade, Wendy, and Kevin lifted it from its grave.

Rut stared down the barrel end.

"Careful, dummy," Wendy said.

He scoffed. "It's full of dirt. It won't go off."

"You gotta be careful anyway," Kevin said. "I've shot my dad's shotgun bunches of times."

Slade took possession of the gun, aimed, and fake fired. "Boom!"

"What are we gonna do with it?" Kevin asked.

The group looked at one another. Two shrugged.

"Play with it, I guess," Slade answered. "Keep it as a souvenir."

"What's that?" Wendy asked.

Slade lowered the weapon. "What's what?"

"That metal part." She pointed to an oval-shaped metal plate on the stock.

Slade spit on it and rubbed the metal. "It's the Rebel flag. The stars part."

"You know what this is?" Kevin said. "It's from the Civil War. It's from that battle that was around here."

"What battle?" Rut asked.

"There was some Civil War battle around here. My dad said Civil War buffs would come back here sometimes with metal detectors and look for stuff."

"There's writin' there too." Wendy took the gun from Slade and lifted the oval plate to her face. "It's a star on the bottom and some words on top. Rrrr . . . sss . . . I can't tell."

"It's a conundrum," Kevin said.

The others looked at him, confused by the word.

Kevin had once won a vocabulary contest in school. The teacher challenged them to find as many of their new vocabulary words as possible in newspapers and magazines and bring them in. The one with the most after a certain period won the contest. On more than one occasion, Kevin's father would pick up his *TV Guide* to find several holes where Kevin had cut out the sentence with one of those new vocabulary words. Kevin won but found disappointment with the prize: a book called *30 Days to a More Powerful Vocabulary*.

Kevin continued, "A conundrum. You know, an enigma."

"What?" Larry said. "Speak English."

Kevin, annoyed, clarified, "It's a mystery. And we have to solve it."

"I know what we can do," Wendy said. "We had this substitute teacher this year in history. Mrs. Oberlin. She told me she would be workin' at the city library all summer. Said I should come by and check out some books for summer readin'."

"Yeah, so?" Rut interrupted.

"Soooo, she taught us all about the Civil War. She knows about this kind of stuff. If anyone knows what this is, she will. We can go see her in the mornin'."

"Yep. We need to go see her," Kevin said.

Slade nodded. "All right. But this is a secret. We'll tell her we found somethin' else. Like a canteen. We'll hide it in that hollowed-out tree."

"Man. This is so cool," Rut said. "Coolest summer ever."

* * *

SETTLED THAT THEY'D accomplished a solid start on the fort, they spent the next two hours with shoes and socks off in the creek. They'd bring better tools the next day. They began the trek back down Devil's Backbone.

Kevin strategically positioned himself in the middle of the line of bikes. As they passed the cemetery and then the Claymore house, he kept a hard stare to his left and avoided making eye contact with the home and anything else that might be there.

CHAPTER 5

F IVE BICYCLES FILLED the rack outside the Mead Creek library the next morning. The teens walked between two columns at exactly 10:00 AM when the library opened. The structure had once housed the post office until the city built a modern structure with new technology. An elderly woman clutched her purse. She was the only other patron awaiting the door to open.

Click!

The lock turned and the door opened.

"Good morning, Mrs. Hamlin," the librarian said to the elderly woman, who visited a minimum of three times per week for her latest romance novel. "And who do we have here?" she said, looking at the five youths.

Wendy offered a curt wave. "Hi, Mrs. Oberlin."

"Oh, Wendy, right?"

"Yes, ma'am."

She placed her hands on her hips. "Well, I must say, I'm very happy to have so many eager readers this early." She spoke in a polite but intelligent Texas drawl.

Twenty-three-year-old Kim Oberlin earned her teaching certificate after four years at Texas A&M University. She married her high school sweetheart, David Oberlin, who served as the First Baptist Church's youth pastor. They lived in one of the two apartment buildings in town and had yet to add to their family.

She wore a summer dress and had her long blond hair pulled behind her ears on each side. She kept eyeglasses in her purse but rarely used them.

Mrs. Oberlin held the doors as each one walked in.

Slade stood, staring at her.

"You coming in?"

"Huh?" Slade recovered and grinned. "Oh, yeah."

She smiled and shook her head.

The post office building turned library smelled old. Musty. Ornate crown molding ran along the edge of the ceiling with cracks every few feet. The group of five kids looked up, down, and sideways at the rows of books. Mead Creek couldn't boast the largest library in East Texas, but the ladies that ran the local Friends of the Library made sure patrons had access to all the classics and that the latest best-sellers made their way to the shelves.

Another, and much older, librarian looked up at Kevin and offered an indifferent nod. She returned to banging on a typewriter as bars struck the paper.

Mrs. Oberlin walked up and rubbed her hands. "So, what can I interest you guys in? *Treasure Island*? *Tom Sawyer*? We just got a new biography of Babe Ruth."

Kevin nudged Wendy.

She looked at him and then at Mrs. Oberlin. "The Civil War."

"Oh. You mean you want to learn about the Civil War?"

"Yes, ma'am," she said curtly.

"How exciting. You should start with Bruce Catton's book. It's a pictorial history of the Civil War, so you can see all the maps and everything. Then, I'd recommend—"

"We just want to learn about that battle that was near here," Kevin said.

"I see. Well, I'm afraid there aren't any books on that. It wasn't exactly a big battle or really even a battle at all. It's more of what military historians would call a skirmish. What makes it so interesting is that the local militia fought off several retreating Federal troops.

"From what I understand, after the Battle of Mansfield in Louisiana, a company of retreating Union troops were lost. They had stopped along Mead Creek to water their horses. The local militia heard they were there and rode out to surprise them."

She seated herself on a table and continued. "The militia won the fight, technically, but the Union troops were able to get away. No one really knows how many casualties there were, but the militia claimed they wounded dozens."

"So, the battle was right out in the woods by Devil's Backbone?" Kevin asked.

She nodded. "Yep. There's a historical marker on the highway. You've probably passed it in your parents' car plenty of times. Tells all about it. When the state first put the marker there, they called it a skirmish. Some of the locals called their friends in Austin to have it replaced by one that said 'the Battle of Mead Creek' as well as a few other changes.

"What's got y'all so interested in this?"

"We found somethin' from the battle!" Rut announced.

The others looked at him, ready to pounce before he uttered the word "shotgun."

Rut tightened his lips.

"We found a canteen," Larry said, matter-of-factly. "We were messin' around back there yesterday, diggin' and stuff. We hit metal and out came this canteen. It had this metal plate on it with a symbol like a Rebel flag."

Slade grinned on one side and lightly nodded in approval of Larry's telling of their deception.

Mrs. Oberlin cocked her head. "Wow! That's quite a find. The Rebel flag symbol is called the Stars and Bars. I've not heard of Civil War canteens having metal identification. Some canteens were wood and some metal. Sometimes they had a cloth covering. Is it wood or metal?"

"Metal," Wendy stated.

"Can I see it?" Mrs. Oberlin asked.

Wendy looked at the others for the answer, then back at the librarian. "Well, we have it in sort of a safe place. Might be worth somethin'. So, we didn't want to carry it around."

"Well. That's good thinking. I know others have found a few Minié balls, you know, like bullets, back there with metal detectors. I guess it's possible someone could have dropped their canteen, and it got buried over time."

"Where's this historical marker?" Kevin asked.

"On the highway. About a mile south of Pollard's Lumber." Mrs. Oberlin picked up a stack of books and placed them on a cart.

Kevin cocked his head in the direction of the door, signaling the others that it was time to go.

They offered a collective "Thanks!" and made their exit.

"You're welcome. Come back anytime. I love talking about this stuff." She turned from the group and began shelving some books.

Kevin noticed an elderly man with long white hair browsing in an aisle.

Slade, the last one out the door, turned back for one more look at the young librarian. He ran his fingers through his hair, feathering it back. "What a fox. I may have to come to the library more often," he said with a smile.

The other boys chuckled.

Wendy rolled her eyes.

———— •◉• ————

THE CREW ROLLED through the alley behind downtown buildings, from the library to the edge of town. They avoided the traffic on Main Street and a potential tongue-lashing from old man Pollard. Two of them carried athletic bags over their shoulders with hammers, nails, and a few other tools they might need for construction.

"Guess what I got in the mail yesterday?" Kevin said to Larry, who rode next to him.

"What?"

"My KISS Army membership," he whispered.

Larry looked over, and said, "KISS Army! Cool!" but failed to keep it to a whisper.

"You joined the KISS Army?" Slade asked. "Why?"

Kevin shrugged. "Just wanted to. Besides, it was only five bucks. Got a membership card, a patch, and some other cool stuff. I love anythin' about KISS."

"Why? Who still likes KISS?" Rut asked.

"I do," Larry answered.

"They're all right I guess. Music's okay. I just don't get the clown makeup," Slade said.

Kevin rolled his eyes. "They wear makeup so no one will know what they look like."

"Why?" Slade asked.

"Because. They want to remain anonymous. You know. Be mysterious. That's what makes them so cool." Kevin nodded, satisfied with his answer.

Larry chimed in, "Yeah . . . I want to see them in concert so bad. Man, that'd be so dang cool. I love KISS *Alive II*. Just like their concert. Best live album ever. 'Shout it, shout it, shout it out—'"

An indignant Slade interrupted. "Man! No way. *Foghat Live*. 'I'm a fool for the city,'" he said, bobbing his head and singing the tune.

"You're both wrong," Wendy said. "Aerosmith. *Bootleg*."

"Ohhh. I'm tellin'. Mom said you're not supposed to listen to devil music," Rut said.

Wendy swerved close to Rut and backhanded his arm. "Shut up. It's not devil music. My friend Katie has it, and her parents go to church just like we do. She's allowed to have it."

"KISS is definitely devil music accordin' to my mom," Slade said with a laugh. "She listens to fifties music. Elvis and stuff. 'That's real rock 'n' roll,' she says."

"Your mom is a religious nut," Kevin said.

Slade shook his head. "Nah. We just go to church and stuff. My mom says it keeps me grounded."

"Pfft. Keeps you from bein' grounded," Kevin said.

"Ha, ha," Slade said. "My Sunday school teacher was talkin' about this a few weeks ago. Said if you play some songs backward, you hear these Satanic messages or somethin' sayin' you should do drugs."

They reached the edge of downtown and turned south toward the historical marker. The lack of buildings, open fields, and two-lane asphalt highway enhanced the noon heat. They immediately moved to the side as a car came from behind them.

"So how do you play a record backward?" Rut asked.

Slade took one hand off the handlebars and mimicked his finger on a record in a circular motion. "You just turn it backward real slow."

"Bull crud," Rut said.

"It's true," Larry added. "We tried it once. I mean, it made sounds, but didn't hear no Satanic messages."

Rut scoffed. "What, like, da, da, da, smoke weed, da, da, da, smoke weed?"

"It said somethin' when we played KISS backward," Slade said, mimicking his finger on a record again. "Kevin. Send us five dollars. Kevin. Send us five dollars."

Four of them laughed.

Kevin didn't. "You suck, Slade."

"I heard that KISS stands for Knights in Satan's Service," Rut said.

Kevin whipped his head toward Rut. "That's bull!"

Rut stuck out his bottom lip and cocked his head. "Just what I heard, man."

"Your parents really won't let you listen to Aerosmith?" Slade asked Wendy.

"She won't let us listen to any rock 'n' roll. Wants us to listen to Neil Sedaka or Glen Campbell. Who wants to listen to that? Ugh." Wendy began to impersonate her mom. "'They don't sing about drugs and sex.' Man, she is so uptight. Says the same stuff to my dad."

"That's why they're gettin' a divorce," Rut said.

Slade, Kevin, and Larry all looked at him, mouths agape.

"Rut!" Wendy said. "They're not gettin' a divorce."

"Are too. Mom keeps yellin' at him for not goin' to church. Says he should be readin' the Bible instead of readin' those westerns. I heard them out in the garage. She said everyone in this house has to go to church and read the Bible. He said somethin' like maybe he won't be in this house much longer. Man, I'm sick of them arguin' all the time. They think we don't hear 'em. I've heard 'em arguin' plenty of times."

Wendy looked at Rut sternly. "But, they aren't gettin' a divorce."

"How come you don't go to church, Kevin?" Slade asked.

Kevin shrugged. "Dunno. We're supposed to be Methodist or somethin', but we don't ever go. My dad gets this newsletter in the mail every month. Guess it's from the church. He always says we should start goin', but we never do, thank God. I'm glad. Sounds borin'. He grew up goin' and said he was christened or somethin' like that. Whenever I get in trouble, my dad says, 'Should've christened the boy.'"

"You should go with us sometime," Larry said.

"Don't y'all go way over in Fairmont?" Rut asked.

"Yeah. My folks don't like the Catholic church here. Don't like the priest so we go over there."

Larry Woodard didn't remember his biological parents. His father's family frowned upon his dad marrying a Mexican woman. His dad used the GI Bill to attend college and met his mom during their senior year. They eloped and graduated, and she was soon pregnant. The two sects refused to yield to one another. Larry's birth brought the extended families together.

As Larry's parents drove home from a well-deserved date, they died in a fiery car crash, leaving the toddler without parents.

His mother's Hispanic parents legally adopted him, raised him in the Catholic faith, and spoke Spanish in the home. They felt it important he keep his father's last name, Woodard, as opposed to Gutierrez. Larry spoke both Spanish and English fluently but hated Lorenzo, as his grandmother called him, and Lawrence as some extended family called him. He'd correct anyone to call him Larry.

He gave Kevin a heartfelt invitation. "Why don't you go to Mass with us sometime?"

"Mass?" Kevin asked.

"Yeah. Church. We call it Mass."

Kevin shrugged. "I dunno. Maybe. Why?"

"Don't you wanna go to Heaven?" Larry asked.

"You can come with me, Kevin," Slade said. "The preacher said we're supposed to invite sinners." He grinned.

Kevin attempted to kick Slade's bike, but Slade swerved. "Butthole!" Kevin said.

They all chuckled.

———————— •◆• ————————

ALL FIVE ROSE up on their bikes for a tough one hundred yards of uphill pedaling.

"Man, this is a lot steeper than I thought," Kevin said.

Slade passed him. "One day, we'll just fly everywhere like on *The Jetsons*. By 1999, they'll probably invent flyin' bikes."

Kevin shook his head. "If they're flyin', then aren't they just planes?"

"Huh?" Slade asked.

"Think about it. I don't even understand why they call them flyin' cars. They fly, so they're just planes."

"Because, dummy, when they're on the ground you drive them like a car," Slade answered.

Kevin grunted through hard pedaling. "If it can fly . . . huh, huh . . . why bother settin' it on the ground? Why not just fly it?"

"Exactly! Why would we be pedalin' if we could just fly it?" Larry said.

"That's what I'm sayin'," Slade said. "They need to invent flyin' bikes."

Kevin shook his head in disgust.

One by one as they reached the peak, they sat for a restful coast downward.

"Where is this thing?" Larry said, breathlessly.

"She said about a mile south. Should be pretty close."

Wendy pointed. "Over there. There's a little gravel drive and a sign."

They looked both ways across the state highway but saw no cars as they pedaled across the road. They stayed on their bikes five across to read the marker.

"I'll read it," Kevin announced. He squinted. "The Battle of Mead Creek. On April 9, 1864, a group of local militia led by E. M. Pollard engaged—"

Rut interrupted. "Pollard! Hey, I wonder if that's the same—"

"Let me just finish," Kevin said. "Engaged a makeshift company of Union regulars retreating from the Battle of Mansfield and resting along Mead Creek, one point two miles east. Using the element of surprise, they attacked the Union camp from two angles. Although outnumbered, the Union troops managed to organize an escape in an eastward direction. They suffered several minor wounds but were able to rejoin the Red River Campaign. The Confederate militia suffered no casualties. Known as Pollard's Raiders, they returned to town victorious but saw no further action during the war."

"Yeah, that's got to be about the Pollard family. Same ones that own the hardware store and lumber yard," Larry said.

"Look at this." Wendy hopped off her bike and let it fall to the gravel. She pointed to the corner of the historical marker. It's the symbol. The same one from the shotgun. There's the Stars and Bars. And it says Pollard's Raiders. You see that? Remember those letters at the bottom we couldn't read? Must have got left behind and just buried over time."

"Not exactly the same," Slade said. "Maybe."

"Whoa! We've got a real live shotgun from the Civil War," Rut declared.

CHAPTER 6

"LET'S GO," KEVIN said. He turned his bike north.

"Wait a minute. Why we goin' that way? I know a shortcut through the woods. We can just ride straight to the fort," Slade said.

Wendy, with hands on hips, asked, "You sure?"

"I'm positive. Just trust me." He pointed south. "There's a road a little bit down, and we can take it almost the whole way. Done it a million times." He pushed his pedal forward, leaving no opportunity for further objections.

The county road, a little more developed than Devil's Backbone, did offer a level and straight shot for half a mile.

"This way," Slade yelled as he veered off onto a trail cutting through thick brush and trees.

The trail opened up and offered a direction toward the fort.

Slightly winded, all four kept up with Slade as he came to an abrupt stop as the trail ended.

"Great. We're lost, aren't we?" Rut said.

"No! Shut up, I'm thinkin'," Slade said, looking left and right. "This way." He headed through tall grass and found what may or may not have been a trail.

The next forty minutes involved more trial and error as they reached a creek.

"See. Told you I'd find it," Slade said.

"First of all, we haven't found the fort. And you don't even know if this is the right creek, genius," Larry said.

"What other creek would it be?" Slade asked

"Yeah, and how we suppose to cross it?" Rut asked.

Kevin, who had ridden a little further down, waved. "Down here. We can cross here."

They dismounted their bikes, removed their shoes and socks, and carried their bikes across the creek. Once they'd settled their bikes on the bank, all five decided to find a seat and wade their feet in the cool, clear water.

Kevin noticed a busy crawdad backing out from beneath a rock.

Larry threw rocks several feet down and added a *plop* to the creek's existing noise with each drop.

Slade stood. "Let's go. We can just walk along the creek 'til we get to the fort."

He took off one way and Kevin the other.

Wendy threw up her arms. "Wait. Which way?"

"This way," Slade and Kevin said in unison but pointing in opposite directions.

"Great," she said. "Too many chiefs, not enough Indians."

"I got us this far, didn't I?" Slade said.

They complied and followed Slade down the creek for nearly ten minutes when all of them, including Slade, sensed he had guessed wrong.

"Tell you what. I'm goin' back the other way," Kevin announced.

They followed him, passing their recent crossing and wading

site, and continued along the creek as it meandered through the woods. With great relief, they found the fort.

Their plan for big breakfasts to tide them over until dinner failed to account for strenuous activity. Their bodies craved fuel and their dry mouths begged for water. They gave in and drank from the creek.

"Just a few mouthfuls. You don't want to get sick," Slade suggested.

"My dad says you shouldn't drink from the creek," Wendy said.

Slade gulped and lifted his face. "That's just if it's dark. As long as it's clear, a little bit won't hurt none."

Wendy made a yuck face as the four boys lapped up water. "I'm not drinkin' that." She licked her dry lips and noticed the oohs and aahs from those that quenched their thirst. She finally dropped to her hands and knees for a swallow. Her pony tail fell forward and dipped into the water.

They managed to get little work done on the fort but did retrieve the shotgun from the hollowed-out tree to study it and rehash what they had learned.

Exhausted, they made their way to Devil's Backbone and rode toward home, speaking little. Family dinner and baseball awaited.

As they passed the Claymore mansion, each of them gave it a cursory glance.

Kevin chose to give it a stern look. Please don't be there. Please don't be there, he thought to himself regarding the face in the window. He looked once and saw no face. No figure. The house looked peaceful and still in the early evening sun. "Phew," he whispered.

"LARRY! WE'VE MADE a gaffe," Kevin said to him as they began their bike ride down the street from their homes.

"Lorenzo! It looks like rain. Don't go too far," his grandmother said in Spanish.

"Okay," he replied, over his shoulder. "Ugh. I hate when she calls me that. Now, what did you say?"

"We made a gaffe about the shotgun."

"Dude. Speak. English. I know you won the big vocabulary contest, but—"

"We screwed up about the shotgun," Kevin said. "I was talkin' to my dad last night about the Civil War. He told me all about the whole Mead Creek battle and how it really wasn't a big deal. I didn't tell him we found somethin' because he'd wanna see it. I just asked him what kinds of guns they used in that battle. He went on and on about muskets, so I asked him about shotguns. He said it was mostly just cavalry units that used them but not that often. You know, they fought on horses. Pretty rare they'd be usin' shotguns."

Larry cocked his head. "So, Pollard's Raiders were cavalry?"

"Don't think so. But it gets weirder. I started askin' him all about kinds of shotguns. He thought it was weird I was askin' so many questions, but he likes to talk about history. He said that the pump shotgun, like the one we found, wasn't even invented durin' the Civil War."

They stopped in front of Slade's house.

His mom watered periwinkle flowers. "Hi, boys." She waved. "Slade! Your little friends are here," she yelled at the house.

Slade opened an upstairs window. He poked his upper body out with no shirt on. "Be right down."

Larry gave him a head nod and looked back to Kevin. "So that gun isn't from the battle?"

"Nope. He got out his shotguns and was showin' me his pump-action and over-and-under. The one we found is pump-action.

So definitely not."

Slade emerged from the garage on his bike.

His mom offered the same warning about rain.

Slade looked up. Clouds filled the air but none seemed too threatening.

They updated Slade on what Kevin had learned and then did the same for Rut and Wendy as they made the trip across downtown.

"So why does it have the Pollard's Raiders thingy on it?" Wendy asked.

Kevin's mouth curled. "That's what we're gonna find out."

— • ● • —

THE SKY RUMBLED and, along with a rolling, darkening cloud, echoed the warnings from Larry's grandmother and Slade's mom. Rut looked up as they crossed the highway, passed through the Pollard's Lumber parking lot, and neared the entrance to Devil's Backbone.

Slade slammed his brakes. "Wait. We gotta get some stuff off that scrap pile. We especially need somethin' for a door."

Although the lumber yard's workers had neatly stacked product for sale inside the fence, this pile had formed from years of workers throwing their scrap over the fence. A few summer weeds jutted up between boards, pallets, and broken glass.

They turned their bikes around and reached the pile. Rummaging through it, they traded turns saying, "What about this?" or "Will this work?"

"Lookin' for somethin'?" A huge, imposing silhouette stood before them, the sun above him peeking through clouds. He wore utility pants with a button-down shirt struggling to remain tucked over his belly. Dozens of keys hung from his belt clip.

They looked back. Caught in the act. No one spoke.

He stepped a little closer. "Well? You kids lookin' for somethin'?" he said in a deep voice. "I mean, don't care none. It's mostly trash. But there's glass and nails and splinters. Don't want y'all gettin' cut up."

"We just need some wood. For a project we're makin' in the woods," Larry said.

"Uh-huh. Well, just be careful. Get what you need but just today. And don't tell no one. I don't want everyone and their dog diggin' through the pile. Somebody'll get a nail in their foot and sue me." He turned and began to walk away.

"Hey, mister. You know the Pollards?" Kevin asked to the astonishment of the others.

"Yeah. Me. I'm a Pollard. Jefferson Pollard."

Kevin pointed to the sign on the highway. "So, this is your lumber yard?"

"It's a family business. There's a bunch of us Pollards. My dad's the mayor."

"Mayor Stump?" Slade suggested.

He chuckled. "Yeah. That's him. Better not let him hear you sayin' that."

Jefferson Pollard's father was the seventy-six-year-old Marty "Stump" Pollard, who earned the nickname for always being on the political stump. His career began as his high school class president, and he later became Mead Creek's youngest mayor at twenty-six. He served multiple terms over several stints. He'd lose on occasion, but after a few months back on the stump, would persuade the townspeople to put him back in office in the next election cycle. At seventy, he had convinced them he was still young and spry enough to hold the office and had kept them convinced the last six years. Unlike his older brother, Ephraim, Stump always wore a smile.

Wendy nudged Kevin. "Ask him about the marker."

"You know that historical marker down the highway a bit? One about the Battle of Mead Creek. Has this Pollard's Raiders thing on it. Ever heard of it?"

Jefferson crossed his arms. "Of course I have. You kiddin'? Heard about it my whole life. Why?"

Kevin shrugged. "Just curious. We were ridin' our bikes down there and read it."

The man pulled a red bandana from his back pocket and rubbed his forehead. A mid-morning summer day in Texas meant the heat had already exacted its toll. Clouds had blocked the sun much of the morning, but the humidity rose to unbearable levels. He turned over a five-gallon metal bucket and took a seat.

Slade, still holding a three-by-four piece of plywood, dropped it and stepped toward the man for his response.

"You read on the sign that the group was led by E. M. Pollard. That was my great-grandpa. Fancied himself quite the military leader. He thought ole General Lee would just make him a general, but he didn't really have no soldierin' experience. He owned the general store in town when the war broke out. He had a bum leg from fallin' off a horse when he was young, so he really couldn't go off to war. But, he was pretty good at organizin' so the locals put him in charge of the local militia. He decided to call himself Major Pollard.

"The militia was mostly men too old to go off to war, and they called themselves Pollard's Raiders. They'd get together on occasion and practice battle drills but figured they'd never get in a fight. Some kid was fishin' in the creek near here when he saw all these Bluecoats."

"Bluecoats?" Rut asked.

"Yankees. Called 'em Bluecoats since they wore blue uniforms.

Like I was sayin', this kid that was fishin' dropped his cane pole and ran all the way back to town and straight into the general store. My great-grandpa was talkin' to some farmer and heard about the Bluecoats. So, he sent the farmer and the kid to get the others to muster up in town. An hour later, they rode out to Mead Creek. No one knows for sure, but we think the fightin' was down there near Meyer's Pond."

Rut elbowed Kevin and whispered, "Right by our fort—uh—project."

He wiped his brow again. "Sounds about right, but who knows? Story has been changed over the years. At first, the Raiders came back sayin' they whipped the Yankees. Some said they killed a bunch of 'em and some said the Yankees just turned tail and ran. Truth is, they likely surprised 'em and fired off a few shots. The Yankees were experienced but battle weary and restin' from a long ride. I think they fought back and were able to ride off before gettin' in too much of a fight. So, I'd like to tell you that legend about my family is true, but truth be told, they startled some Yankees and ran 'em off."

"That's it?" Slade said, disgusted.

"That's it," Jefferson said with a chuckle. He stood, re-tucked his shirt, and pulled up his pants. "Sorry to disappoint, but that's about it. Pollard's Raiders never amounted to much. That symbol you saw on the historical marker was about all they had. Some of them put 'em on patches for their coats and hats or made plaques on their wall. They put it on other stuff, but everyone forgot about 'em several years after the war.

"My grandpa inherited the store and turned it into just a hardware store and started this lumber company. My dad, you know, Mayor Stump," he said, smiling, with his hand cupped as if telling them a secret, "and my Uncle Ephraim kept the business goin' and growin'. Now I pretty much run it."

He walked off and without turning said, "Remember, take what you want today, but don't tell nobody."

"Thank you!" Kevin said.

Jefferson threw up a wave. "Welcome."

———•◉•———

KEVIN PREPARED FOR his "to look or not to look" decision as they neared the Claymore mansion on the way to the fort.

A bright streak raced across the sky.

Crack!

The thunder, one second later, caused all five to duck their heads and shoulders.

The sky had drawn increasingly dark the last several minutes. As they rode, the giant drops fell on and around them.

Slade kept the lead, undeterred.

The drops turned heavy, and a haze of rain came toward them.

"Quick! Over here!" Slade led them under a clump of trees that allowed little rain through.

They enjoyed the protection from the elements but not the view. The Claymore house stood across the way.

Kevin turned, looking into the woods.

The others studied it and pondered.

"I bet it's haunted," Rut offered.

"Shut up," his sister said. "Don't say that. It's just some old house. No one even lives there. Looks like it's about to fall over." She turned and stood next to Kevin, looking away from the old home.

Wind blew water nearly horizontal as the storm picked up. They covered their faces as rain swept in under the canopy of the trees, and they forgot about the house. Three minutes later, the storm let up. Clouds covered the sky, but the rain had reduced to sprinkling.

"Watch me hawk this loogie." Slade snorted, coughed, and spit a giant wad of mucus fourteen feet, just missing the trunk of a tree he'd aimed for. Whether a cold in the winter or allergies in the summer, he always seemed ready to produce the requisite phlegm for adequate spitting ammunition. He could also curl his tongue, providing a ramp for the missile.

"Ew. Gross!" Wendy said.

Rut smiled in appreciation. He tried to hawk one, but it fell only feet in front of him.

Larry stepped out from under the tree. "Man, it's just gonna keep rainin'. No baseball tonight."

"I ain't ridin' through all that mud, and it's just gonna keep on rainin'," Wendy said. She pulled her shirt out to shake out the moisture.

"Screw that, it'll be fun," Slade said.

"Nah. Let's go to my house and play Monopoly," Larry said. "We got all summer to be out here."

Slade picked up his bike. "All right, losers. Let's just go. But we need to come back tomorrow. Bring food and water. And stay after dark. No baseball tomorrow. We can just tell our parents we're at each other's houses. They won't check, and we can stay late."

"Yeah!" Rut said.

"I dunno," Kevin said. "What do you think, Larry?"

"Sounds good to me," he answered. "We just say we're playin' hide-and-seek at the park real late. That way they won't check at our houses."

"I'm in," Wendy said.

"Okay, cool. We can finish up the fort, build a fire, and cook hot dogs," Slade said.

"Yeah. And bring back stuff we need, like chairs and stuff," Larry said.

"What about this stuff we got off the scrap pile?" Kevin asked.

Slade threw his board down. "Leave it. Who's gonna take it?"

Kevin dropped his board and looked at the house. Maybe the ghost in that house, he thought.

CHAPTER 7

WITH THEIR ELABORATE cover stories in place and supplies in backpacks, the group returned to the tree across from the Claymore mansion near twenty-four hours later.

Slade picked up the piece of plywood that would serve as their door. A difficult item to carry while riding a bike, but he managed. He laid it across his back and grabbed the edge to hold on.

Larry cocked his head, looking at Slade's board. "Weren't those nails stickin' out?"

Slade lowered it and noticed the nails were bent over and flush with the wood. "Huh. Nah. Must have been like this. Can't remember."

They arrived at the fort expecting a muddy mess, but the Texas sun had quickly dried up the heavy showers, and thick trees spared their camp the worst of the storm.

The fort itself measured six feet by eight and more resembled a shanty. The roof stood six feet tall at its highest point but slanted down several inches. Essentially, they'd made a box. Kevin gave out several orders on where to put a particular board and how many nails to hammer in. They all ignored him and hammered away. There was no craftsmanship. Hardly the elaborate structure Kevin had drawn up, but they had finished it.

They managed to work the flat pieces or cut holes so that each side had a window, but they had no glass. The windows simply opened to the air. They needed them, as the temperature in the mid-afternoon climbed to near one hundred degrees. The fort rested under a heavy clump of trees, so they enjoyed the full shade, and a light breeze made it bearable inside. Regardless, kids don't concern themselves with temperature like adults do.

Three sides showed remains of red paint that the wood had a long time ago when it served another structure. The fourth side had the red on the inside.

"Y'all realize this side is on backwards?" Wendy asked.

Kevin and Slade inspected.

Kevin shrugged. "We'll repaint later anyway."

Rut had lugged three folding camping stools he stole from his garage. Two buckets found in the woods rounded out seats for all five.

Kevin brought a small KISS poster that he had acquired from his latest issue of *Circus* magazine and taped it inside.

Slade posted up Cheryl Tiegs in a pink bikini. It had hung on his bedroom wall for four days until his mom discovered it while vacuuming. She didn't rip it down, but when his dad got home, the order came forth.

"Son. Posters like that belong on garage walls. Not yours. Get rid of it."

Slade drooped his shoulders. "Yes, sir."

He hid it in their backyard shed and had waited for an opportunity to proudly display it.

Larry and Wendy thought practically. He brought a big jug of water and hot dogs. She contributed candles and a Bic lighter.

As evening approached, and content with a finished product,

the five settled into their new abode.

"What are we gonna name it?" Rut asked.

Larry and Kevin looked at one another, realizing they hadn't thought about it.

"Fort Kickass," Slade announced. "We want it to sound tough."

Wendy, her face buried in a *Teen Beat* magazine, shook her head. Without looking up, she offered, "How about Fort Unicorn?"

"What? Shut up," Slade said.

She lowered her magazine. "I'm kiddin'. Why even call it a fort? I just don't get it. I mean, do ya think Indians are gonna shoot arrows at us?"

Kevin nodded. "Yeah. We were callin' it a fort. It's more of a clubhouse. Just a place to hang out."

Wendy nodded in approval and returned to her magazine with Scott Baio on the cover.

Kevin grinned a little. Careful that the other boys wouldn't notice. He wanted Wendy's approval. He wanted her there. He just didn't want the other boys to know that.

"What we need to call it is a codename. You know. So we can talk about it without others knowin'," Larry said.

"Good idea," Slade said. "How about Golden somethin'? Like from James Bond."

"No, no, no," Kevin said. "That would just make someone suspicious. Just a name. Like Alfalfa. We could say we're goin' to Alfalfa's."

"Oh, yeah. There's plenty of Alfalfas around here. That wouldn't be suspicious at all," Slade said.

"Why don't you just call it 'the Creek'?" Wendy said, again without looking up. "That way no one will know what we're talkin' about, or exactly where. But we'll know."

All four boys looked at one another, smiling.

"That's perfect," Larry announced. "All in favor of callin' it the Creek say aye."

"Aye," they said in unison.

Wendy twirled an indifferent finger and said, "Aye, aye."

Kevin squinted at her magazine.

Slade noticed. "You need glasses. You're always squintin'."

"No, I don't," Kevin said. "I can just squint. I ain't wearin' glasses." He squinted again. "What are you readin'?" he asked Wendy.

Rut pointed at the cover and poked Scott Baio's face. "She's probably readin' about him." He made kissing sounds.

Slade laughed.

She backhanded his arm. "Shut up, turd."

"You're so in love with him." Rut made more kissing sounds. She raised a hand and he winced to protect himself.

Larry stood. "We better gather firewood before it gets dark." He pushed on the door to open it. They had managed to attach hinges, but the door operated on more of a sliding out method.

Each of them ventured several yards into the woods, gathering pieces they deemed useful.

Wendy noticed Slade and Larry facing away from her and slightly ajar to one another. She heard the distinct sound of liquid hitting the ground. "Uh, excuse me! You just take a leak wherever you want?"

Larry, slightly startled, did his best to finish.

Slade had no concerns with modesty. "Hey, when you're in the woods the bathroom is everywhere. Gotta let it fly."

"Well, I need to go," she said, arms folded.

"Well, go," Slade said, over his shoulder. "Just pick a spot."

She looked left and right. "Rut!" she yelled.

"What?" He dropped his armful of dead branches near the fort.

"I need to go. You have to come stand watch."

Slade zipped. "No one's gonna look. Just go."

"C'mon," Kevin said, elbowing Rut. "We'll stand watch."

Wendy, Kevin, and Rut made their way from the creek bed toward the clearing and near the edge of their entrance from Devil's Backbone.

She found a tree trunk much wider than her and walked around it. "You watch that way, and you watch the other."

They both nodded, taking their job seriously.

Wendy began to squat and decided she was still a little too close. She didn't want anyone to hear her doing her business. She walked farther down the clearing.

Kevin and Rut's conversation turned to mumbling as she moved farther.

Satisfied she had reached a safe distance, she relieved herself. As she stood, she heard a crunching sound and then three snorts. She turned to find a wild hog staring back.

The feral animals occupied much of East Texas despite efforts to curtail their growth with year-round hunting. They weren't dangerous unless wounded, or unless a sow protecting her piglets felt threatened.

At first, the hog didn't look at her. It sniffed and nudged through weeds and twigs.

She took a step back and, on the second step, broke a branch.

The hog noticed and looked up. It made a step for her.

She froze.

Thump! Squeeeel!

At first, she thought someone had thrown a long stick at the hog. Then, as it fell over, she realized an arrow had passed through the animal's midsection.

Indians? she thought.

It hit the ground and its eyes closed.

She backed up three more steps, turned, and ran. She slowed as she approached the two boys. "C'mon. Let's get back."

"What was that noise?" Rut asked.

"Nothin'. C'mon. Let's get back," she said.

They followed, having done their duty.

Slade and Larry formed rocks for a campfire when they returned.

"What's wrong with you?" Larry said to Wendy.

The others looked at her, noticing her normally confident demeanor had changed.

Wendy never wanted the boys to think any less of her. That she couldn't handle any situation they might face. That she didn't belong as much as any of the boys. She didn't want them to think a wild hog scared her. She would have braved her way through that. But the arrow piercing its torso, from the bow of an unseen shooter, rattled her.

Her hand shook as she smoothed her hair behind her ear.

Kevin touched her elbow. "Wendy! What's wrong?"

"A pig. There was a pig back there."

Slade stood. "Cool. You saw a pig? I hear there's a bunch of 'em out here."

"It's dead."

"Dead?" Kevin asked.

"Someone killed it. Right in front of me. I had just finished . . . you know . . . and there was this pig right there. I thought it was gonna attack me. And next thing you know, an arrow went through it." She used her finger to mimic the arrow's path.

"You serious?" Rut asked.

She gave an oh-yeah nod.

"Cool! Let's go check it out," Slade said.

Kevin held him back. "Wait. That means someone else is out

here."

"Yeah. So? People do come out here."

"Yeah, but with bows and arrows?"

"I'll get the shotgun," Rut said, starting to run off.

"To do what?" Larry said. "Not like it shoots."

Rut stopped. "I don't know. Scare someone off maybe."

"People hunt out here. So what? They might've not even seen her. Probably wouldn't have even shot if they saw her. Just saw some pig. I'm goin'," Slade said.

The other four followed.

Wendy moved to the front. "You don't even know where it was. I'll show you."

They reached the spot but found no hog.

"It was right here. I swear!" she said.

"Yeah. Sure. Nice prank," Slade said.

She palmed her face.

The boys began walking off except for Kevin. He inspected a little closer. "Look! Blood. A bunch of it."

The boys returned to see bright red blood puddled on the dirt.

"Told ya," Wendy said. "Maybe the hunter carried it off."

The five stood in a circle around the kill site. No words at the death that had just occurred.

The sun had disappeared behind the tree line with darkness close behind.

Larry waved. "C'mon. We better get the fire started."

Kevin took one look across the clearing but saw no one.

CHAPTER 8

IT TOOK THEM three tries to realize their Bic lighters would not work on wet, green branches to produce a fire.

Slade's father, a smoker, had several lighters lying around the house, so Slade acquired a green one, which he kept for himself.

They managed to find drier wood, and Wendy volunteered a few pages of her magazine for tinder. They each contributed pokes and blows until the flame endured. They certainly didn't need the warmth. Rather, they wanted the success of fire-making.

Slade reached into his backpack and pulled out a half-empty pack of Marlboro Reds. Without saying a word, he tapped one out of the pack, popped it into his mouth, and lit it.

All four of them stared.

"What are ya doin'?" Wendy said with a disapproving tone.

"Borrowed 'em from my dad." He extended the pack. "Anybody else want one?"

Larry reached for one, then Rut.

"You won't tell?" Rut asked Wendy.

She shrugged. "Suit yourself."

Slade had only coughed once and Larry a couple of times.

Rut had a stronger reaction but persevered.

Kevin bowed to peer pressure and lit one.

Slade took a deep drag. "I like a good smoke."

"Fine. Give me one," Wendy said. She coughed as much as Rut. "This is nasty." Her face showed her disgust.

"You're just not used to it," Slade said. "Just keep tryin'."

"Like you smoke all the time," Wendy said.

Slade smiled. "Let's just say the old man doesn't miss one or two now and then. Plus, he'll stub one out when there's plenty of good smoke left on it."

"Gross! You dig 'em out of the ashtray?" Wendy asked.

Slade smiled.

For a few minutes, no one spoke as they toyed with the varying ways to blow smoke out, looked at the ember, and studied the habit.

"Check this out." Slade blew on his ember to clear ashes. He reversed the cigarette with the burning end in his mouth and blew. A steady stream of smoke came out of the filter. He lifted his eyebrows. "Pretty cool, huh? It's called a shotgun."

"I'll try it," Rut announced. He reversed his, coughed, and quickly pulled it as ashes landed on his tongue. "Yuck!"

Kevin sucked in, didn't inhale, and blew out smoke. "My uncle smokes those kind with no filter. Taps 'em on his watch to pack it. Smokes like three packs a day."

"So, what are we gonna do with the gun?" Slade asked. "Might be worth a couple hundred bucks. We can split it five ways. I could use the money."

"For what?" Wendy asked.

He pondered. "The arcade. I could go every day for the whole summer with that much money."

"No way!" Kevin threw his half-smoked cigarette in the fire. "We ain't sellin' it until we figure out where it came from."

Larry nodded. "Yeah. Don't you wanna find out why a shotgun

was buried out here?"

Slade shrugged.

—•◉•—

THE FIRE BURNED brightly as they stuck hot dogs on sharpened sticks and watched them curl. Without any buns or condiments, and chased by swigs of warm water from the jug, the meal seemed less than satisfying. But the idea of being on their own and outside of parental control appealed to their sense of adventure.

Slade held out the pack. "Anybody want another smoke?"

None accepted the offer and he put them away.

Rut smiled and then giggled.

"What's so funny?" Larry asked.

Rut giggled again.

Wendy sniffed and closed her eyes. "Oh, gross!" She back-handed his arm and pulled her shirt over her nose.

The other three boys followed suit with sounds of disgust and sought the protection of their shirts from Rut's flatulence.

"Silent, but deadly," Rut said, smiling.

"He should be in the *Guinness Book of World Records* for that," Wendy said through her shirt.

After a moment of recovery, Slade smiled, looked at Wendy, and then Kevin. "Y'all ever hear of the hook killer?"

"The what?" Rut asked.

"The hook killer. He stalked people in the woods."

Rut's mouth dropped open.

"He's just tryin' to scare you, Rut. It's not true," Wendy said.

Slade leaned back. "How do you know?"

"Scary story around a campfire. Very original," she said.

Slade leaned in. "This couple was in the woods makin' out." He spoke in a slow, methodical voice.

"Where?" Rut interrupted.

"I don't know. Over near Dallas, I think," Slade said, annoyed. He continued in the slow voice, "This couple was makin' out in their car along an abandoned road. Just like Devil's Backbone. The song on the radio stopped and the announcer said a dangerous killer had just escaped from an insane asylum. He was known as the hook killer because he would hang his victims on hooks like meat. He was a butcher or somethin'. The girl got scared and said, 'Maybe we should go.' The boyfriend talked her out of it and they started makin' out again.

"Just then, they hear a scrapin' sound. Just like a hook scrapin' on the car. The boyfriend tells her to stay put while he checks it out. She starts bitin' her nails and then she hears her boyfriend screamin'. She looks back but can't see anythin'. Worst of all, he took the keys with him. She keeps hearin' more scrapin'. It sounds like it's right on the hood of the car. An hour goes by but she doesn't move. Paralyzed by fear."

Knock! Knock! Knock!

All four jumped as Slade knocked on a piece of scrap wood.

"It was a cop. He motioned for her to roll down her window. 'Ma'am. You need to come with me.'

"She told the cop about her boyfriend, but he still said for her to come with him.

"As they walked off, he said, 'Don't look back. Trust me. Do. Not. Look. Back.'

"She got ten feet and looked back anyway. Her boyfriend was hangin' upside down from a giant tree next to the car. He had a great big hook stuck through his chest and his fingernails were scrapin' the roof of the car."

Rut's eyes widened.

"Dang," Kevin said.

Slade leaned back in contentment.

Wendy rolled her eyes.

"That's a good one," Larry said. "Anyone else know a scary story?"

Rut smiled. "You know what I hear is out in these woods? I hear—"

"Don't you dare say Bigfoot," Wendy said. "If you even think of talkin' about that, I'm gonna kick your butt."

Rut shrugged. "All right."

"My grandparents' basement is haunted," Kevin said.

"Nuh-uh," Rut said.

"Oh, yeah. Ya see, they only have one bathroom, and it's in the basement. They live on a farm up in South Dakota where my dad grew up. We go up there sometimes for vacation. They used to just have an outhouse but they put a toilet in the basement like a bunch of years ago. So, when you have to go, you have to go down in the basement.

"One time, when I was a kid, I went down there by myself. It's real cold and dark. And smells old. Each step creaks as you walk down. I was down there, you know, takin' care of business. I looked over my shoulder to the corner. There's this big tarp that hangs from the ceilin'."

"What's behind it?" Wendy asked.

"That's just it. I don't know. I turned back. I felt this real cold feelin' and heard this whoosh sound. I was afraid to look back in that direction. Afraid of what I might see. The whole time, I'm still goin', if you know what I mean. Then, I heard these sounds like someone was walkin' toward me."

Rut raised his eyebrows.

Wendy swallowed.

"I finished and zipped up but was afraid to turn around. I

flushed, closed my eyes, and ran toward where I thought the stairs were. But, I was too afraid to open my eyes. I picked the right spot and just fell down on the steps. I went flyin' up the stairs, like on all fours, and busted through the door. My grandma was there stirrin' somethin' in a pot on the stove. She said, 'You okay, sweetie?' I just nodded.

"Man, that was the most scared I've ever been."

"So what did you do for the rest of the trip?" Larry asked.

"What do you mean?" Kevin asked back.

"Goin' to the bathroom."

"Oh. My younger cousin was stayin' there and I talked him into goin' down with me. Turns out he was scared too. We sorta made a pact."

"Weren't you curious what was behind the tarp?" Wendy asked.

"Yep. But I wasn't gonna look. That was a couple of years ago, and we haven't been back since." As scary as that had been, Kevin hadn't actually seen a ghost, like he had at the Claymore house. In that moment, he almost spoke up about the face. Rut looked at Wendy and said, "Tell 'em your story. The one about the twin beds."

She shivered. "No way. Too scary." She appeared timid.

"C'mon, I told mine," Kevin said.

"All right," she said.

Rut nodded in approval. "This is a good one."

She nodded toward Kevin. "Kinda like you, our family went to go visit relatives up in Oklahoma a few years ago. Like my mom's great uncle and aunt or somethin'. They had this real big house with extra bedrooms, so they said we could each have our own room. This aunt took Rut to his room and then she got me. I was kinda excited to have this whole, giant room to myself. When we got there, it had two twin beds. I looked around and it had all these old photos and other old stuff. Like, antiques.

"She started to pull down the covers of one of the beds and was tellin' how nice it was we came to visit and all that. 'Here we go. Your bed's all ready.' She stopped by the other bed and stared at it. Then she says, 'You don't want to sleep in this bed. My cousin died in that one last year. Tsk, tsk. So tragic.'"

"Holy crap!" Slade said.

"I know. She just said, 'Nighty night,' and walked out." Wendy mimicked the aunt with a curt smile and wave. "There I was stuck in this room where some old person had died. And not just died. Died tragically. What the heck did that mean?"

"So what happened?" Slade asked.

"Well, I got in bed and covered up. No way I was lookin' at the other bed. It was hot, and I was sweatin' but I covered up anyway. It was like I had to sleep with a ghost in the bed next to me. It was so scary. I finally fell asleep. When I woke up, I had kinda forgotten about it. Then I remembered. I looked over at the bed and the covers were all pulled back. Like someone had slept there. A chill ran down my spine. I wanted to scream.

"I ran to the door and opened it. My mom was standin' right there about to walk in. She asked what was wrong, and I told her. She just chuckled and said she slept there. She said her and my dad had one of their fights, so she came and slept there. Still. It was scary."

"Tell them the other part," Rut said.

"What? Oh, yeah. That house we stayed at looks just like the Claymore mansion."

"Yep. Just like it. Except I bet there really are ghosts in the Claymore house," Rut announced.

Kevin dropped the stick he had used to poke the fire. At that moment, he realized what he'd seen at the Claymore house had been confirmed. The ghosts were surely the victims of the heinous crime that had occurred there. He also realized that their trip home would, yet again, have them travel by the Claymore house but this time in the dark.

"Ghosts! What are you talkin' about?" Larry asked Rut.

"I kinda forgot about it, but a few weeks ago, we went to Dairy Queen with our mom for lunch. We sat by all those old men. One of 'em started talkin' about some murder he read about in the paper. Then another one said it reminded him of the Claymore house murders."

"It's true," Wendy said.

Rut continued. "He started sayin' that this whole family was killed and ghosts haunt the house and cemetery. My mom overheard and told us to not listen. She made us get up and move to another table so we didn't hear any more."

"I never heard about that before," Larry said.

"I know," Wendy said. "I tried to get my mom to tell me what she knew about it, but she just said these things aren't discussed. But I wonder how much of that is made up. I want to know what really happened there."

"You know who'll be able to tell us about it? Mrs. Oberlin at the library. We should go ask her." Kevin waved a finger at his idea.

"Yeah. Let's go tomorrow," Wendy said.

"Can't. It's Sunday," Kevin said. "Monday. Ten o'clock."

They all nodded in agreement.

"It's gettin' late. I'm supposed to be home by eleven," Larry said. "We should be goin'."

They all stood and kicked dirt on the fire. Smoke rose as it extinguished. The sudden darkness occurred to them.

"Who brought a flashlight?" Slade asked.

They looked at one another, realizing no one had.

After walking their bikes cautiously from the fort, they reached the clearing. A nearly full moon greeted them, offering just enough light to see along Devil's Backbone.

Kevin, forgetting his normal routine to ride safely in the middle of the pack, brought up the rear of the line of bikes. They quickly rode past the Claymore house. With the talk of ghosts from Rut, his inquisitive mind took over. He wanted to look. He stopped pedaling and coasted. He looked over his shoulder at the darkened house. He looked up at the window where the figure had looked back. Slowly, the room illuminated.

CHAPTER 9

MONDAY MORNING SAW few library patrons other than one lady scanning books in a dusty aisle and one college-aged student scribbling furiously on paper with several stacks of books surrounding him.

"Back again? More Civil War questions?" Mrs. Oberlin asked, her hand on her hip.

Slade ran late, so the other four gave one another that "who'll be our spokesman?" look.

Kevin leaned in. "It's kind of a secret."

Mrs. Oberlin's eyes widened. "Oh," she said, with a patronizing tone. She looked around and noticed that neither patron nor her older co-worker lifted a head at the teens' arrival.

She curled a finger for them to follow her toward the reference section where she sat on a table, crossed her legs, and smoothed out her dress. "Okay. Tell me this secret."

The front door burst open and Slade rushed in. "I'm here!"

Everyone turned toward him.

The older librarian cocked her head with a stern look and shushed him.

He offered a conciliatory hand wave and joined his friends.

Kevin and the others turned back to Mrs. Oberlin.

Slade offered a smile.

"So, is this about the canteen?" Mrs. Oberlin asked, smiling.

"It's about the Claymore mansion down Devil's Backbone," Kevin said. "We ride our bikes past there sometimes and heard there was some murder there a bunch of years ago. You know anythin' about it?"

Her smile subsided. "Yes. Actually, I know a lot about it. It was a terrible, terrible thing. So sad." She looked out the window for a few seconds and turned back. Her optimistic demeanor waned. "Tell you what. Why don't you read about it?" She hopped off the table and walked over to a machine on a desk and tapped it. "You can read about it on microfilm. Have a seat."

Kevin took a seat in front of the machine, which had a large screen and several knobs. Wendy sat next to him. Slade, Larry, and Rut stood behind them.

Mrs. Oberlin knelt to a tiny file drawer and opened it to reveal several small boxes. "These are rolls of microfilm. They're like film negatives of newspapers." She pulled out a box marked *Mead Creek Daily Register*—April to Sept 1912" and pointed to the label. "This is every copy of the newspaper during that time." She proceeded to load the film and show them how to advance the roll.

"Oh, yeah. We learned about microfiche in school last year," Rut said.

"Microfiche are slides. These rolls are microfilm. Very similar," she said.

The screen lit up.

"Wow! Look at those funny hats. And only two bucks," Wendy said, pointing to an ad.

Mrs. Oberlin grinned. "You'll notice a lot of things like that. But, here is where you want to start." She stopped the film on the newspaper's front page for Tuesday, June 4, 1912. "Something tells me you may want to keep reading, so just roll to the next day." She walked back over to the cabinet and pointed at another drawer. "Here, you'll find the same thing for the *Dallas Times Herald*. We even have the New York newspapers from that time. It was a national story for a couple of days."

Kevin read the headline. "Murder at the Claymore Estate."

"You should probably get your parents' permission to read all of this. But, I guess it is our town's history. Just so you know, it's a horrific story."

Rut's mouth dropped, and the others looked at her with stern faces.

She walked away, leaving them to their research and inquiring minds.

Kevin squinted and moved his face toward the screen. He read slowly. "Local farmer Ralph Temple made a gruesome—"

"I'll read it," Wendy said. "You're practically blind. "Local farmer Ralph Temple made a gruesome discovery Monday morning on his way to town. A body lay prone in the yard near the front door of the Claymore mansion.

"'I just knew it was Claymore. He always wore brown trousers and a vest. At first, I thought maybe he'd had a heart attack,' Temple said. He dismounted his horse for a closer inspection.

"As Temple approached the body, his horse jerked its head away, forcing him to pull the reins tight. Blood soaked the dead man's torso. His arms rested straight out from his body, wide open. Temple stated that he looked left and right but saw no one. He mounted his horse and made a dash to town for the sheriff.

"He returned with Sheriff Brown, a deputy, and two local businessmen that had hunting rifles slung over their shoulders. Revolver at the ready, Sheriff Brown knelt beside the body and confirmed the dead man was, indeed, local prosecutor Richard Claymore.

"Temple stayed by the road and reminded them of Claymore's wife and two children. The sheriff ordered the two with rifles to stand guard outside as he and the deputy entered the house.

"At the end of the long hall past the stairs, they noticed two feet in lady's shoes pointed downward. They approached with caution and found a body in a white dress lying face down. They turned her over to find the face nearly blown away. They assumed it to be Claymore's wife, Clara."

"Holy crap!" Kevin said.

Rut turned his head and covered his eyes as if watching a scary movie.

Wendy continued, "Next, they checked each room downstairs but found no one. They headed upstairs, taking each step slowly. In the second bedroom of the second floor, they found the ten-year-old daughter, Ruth. She sat in the corner in a pink dress covered in blood. Her lifeless body clutched a doll. The doll's dress was drenched in blood just like the doll's owner."

"Dang. Who in the world would do this?" Larry asked.

Kevin shook his head. "Man."

Wendy shushed them. "The sheriff and deputy cleared the rest of the house and outbuildings. They found no culprit or murder weapon, nor did they find the thirteen-year-old son, Dickie Claymore.

"Sheriff Brown organized a dozen men to scour the area for Dickie, any clues, and the murderer. The woods surrounding the Claymore estate are thick with brush but open up along Mead Creek. The search continued until dark Monday evening, but no trace of anything relevant to the investigation was discovered as of press time.

"Sheriff Brown refused further comment other than to say he'd work night and day until the murderer was apprehended. When asked how the victims died, he only said, 'We'll get into that later.' An unnamed source that helped remove the bodies stated that all three had suffered gunshot wounds at close range.

"But what of Dickie Claymore? Was he taken? Was this some kidnapping scheme gone bad? Perhaps Dickie is wounded and wandering the woods all alone. Anyone with information is encouraged to visit the sheriff's office.

In the meantime, more than one resident said he'd sleep with a gun at his side.

"That's it," Wendy said.

Slade made a turning motion with his hand. "Go to the next day."

Larry, Slade, and Rut had pulled up chairs as all five huddled around the microfilm reader.

Kevin advanced the film to the *Mead Creek Daily Register*'s next headline.

"No clues in Claymore murder," Wendy read aloud. "Just more of the same."

"Keep lookin'. Down further," Kevin said.

"Listen to this. It's about the Claymores," she said. "Richard Claymore served as the Princeton County district attorney and tried most of his cases in Mead Creek, the county seat. A native Texan, he attended law school back East where he met his wife, Clara. Citing a call to leave the wiles of the big city, they chose to raise their children in a small town much like the one where he had been raised.

"They arrived eight years prior with two small children. Thanks to Clara's inheritance, they purchased twenty-four acres along Mead Creek, hired help to build their large home, and paid for grading of the dirt road from near downtown to their home."

"I bet that dirt road is Devil's Backbone," Kevin said.

"Ya think!" Slade said.

"Ladies in town found Clara a refined woman with elegant tastes. Afternoon teas in the home were well-attended affairs. The family was active at Memorial Methodist Church and had attended services the morning of the murders.

"DA Claymore's first major case involved the prosecution of Marshall Pollard for manslaughter—"

"Whoa, a Pollard," Slade said.

Wendy looked at Slade with widened eyes. "Marshall Pollard for manslaughter. Pollard had a long feud with local banker F. L. Mankin over a failed loan deal. Mankin claimed Pollard lied about his collateral and wasn't shy about spreading that rumor all over town. Pollard approached Mankin on the street and challenged him to a fight, harkening to days of the Wild West. Neither carried guns, but Pollard beat Mankin to death with a pickaxe from his store.

"Pollard had many friends in Mead Creek, but Claymore shrewdly kept them off the jury and easily secured a conviction. Pollard was sent to Huntsville for a thirty-year term. He died in prison of tuberculosis.

"DA Claymore had tried numerous successful cases over the last eight years and sent many a criminal to the penitentiary."

"Did they solve it?" Kevin asked. He rolled the microfilm to each of the next few days with more Claymore murder headlines, but each report repeated the facts of the last.

"Man! Blew the mom's face off. What kind of maniac did this?" Rut asked.

Kevin scrolled to the headline three days after the murder. "Check this out. Says, 'Claymore son found.'"

"Where'd they find him?" Wendy moved in toward the screen and read again, "A father and son fishing in Mead Creek startled someone on the bank rocking back and forth.

"'Are you that Claymore boy?' the father asked.

"The young man nodded without saying a word.

"Dickie Claymore had been found still wearing his Sunday best, although it was torn and soiled.

"The fisherman took Dickie to his home four miles east of Mead Creek where his wife cleaned him up and attempted to feed him. Dickie refused to eat or speak. He brought the Claymore orphan to Mead Creek by wagon and turned him over to the sheriff.

"The street filled with onlookers curious to see what had happened. What had the boy seen? Where had he been for three days?

"That's it. Just more of what we already know," Wendy said.

"Let's go to the next day," Kevin said. He scrolled but found no new information. He tried again. "Here we go."

Wendy covered her mouth as she began to read Dickie's version of events. "He was in his room reading, as his mother required the children to read two hours per day. He heard his father arguing with someone outside. As he walked to the window to see, he heard a gunshot. Dickie fell and scurried back. He then heard commotion in the house, followed by his mother's scream and another gunshot. He ran to a room in the back of the house and climbed out the window and onto the roof. As he shimmied down a pipe connected to the side of the house, he heard the third gunshot.

"Reaching the edge of the woods behind his house, he looked back to see three figures run in the other direction. He didn't see any of his family and hoped that they had survived. When he thought it was safe, he returned home and saw that all three had perished.

"He spent the next several days walking in the woods, ashamed that he didn't stay in the house and defend his family. He had lost track of time and thought he'd better hide in the woods in case the killers returned.

"Dr. Perkins examined Dickie Claymore and said he suffered from shock and was not in a proper state of mind.

"Sheriff Brown stated that Dickie would live with him and his wife until other arrangements could be made."

The five looked through several more days of newspapers and loaded the ones from the Dallas and New York papers. The murder remained unsolved as of the end of that summer. Several articles spoke of experts coming to town to help with the investigation. Detectives had exhausted all leads. There were no witnesses, other than Dickie Claymore.

He had repeated his story dozens of times with no variation. Each time he broke down, telling of his return to the home and finding his father, mother, and sister brutally murdered.

They all sat in silence at what they had just read.

Mrs. Oberlin walked up. "I guess you weren't expecting all that. Maybe I should have warned you."

Kevin placed a microfilm box in the drawer and shut it. "So, did the murder ever get solved?"

"No. Still a mystery as to who murdered that poor family." Mrs. Oberlin shook her head. "No locals seemed the type to do this, so they assumed it was some crazy persons from out of town. Maybe some gang after their riches.

"There was even one theory that Dickie did it. But most everyone agreed that he couldn't have done such a heinous crime. He had no motive. He had no access to the weapon. He acted nothing like a cold-blooded killer that would do such a thing. He was known as a good-natured boy, a strong student.

"His mother, Clara, was an only child and her parents had passed, so Sheriff Brown adopted him, and Dickie lived in town with them. The murders were the talk of the town for years. People would see Dickie, point, and say, 'Tsk, tsk.'

"The house sat empty for years. Mr. Claymore had drawn up a will, and Dickie would inherit the home and several thousand dollars when he turned eighteen. Like many young men his age, he went off to fight in World War I. The distraction of the war caused people to move on. I guess Dickie moved on too."

CHAPTER 10

THEY STRADDLED THEIR five bikes, lined up as if in parking spots, in front of the Claymore home. It seemed peaceful in the early afternoon. Towering trees stood over the property, and the kids found shade as they sat on their bikes and pondered the horrific events that had occurred there sixty-seven years prior. They gazed at the house sitting fifty yards back from the Devil's Backbone road.

A strong breeze offered some relief from the Texas heat. A branch tapped a side window as if knocking to come in. The unkempt nature of the property appeared far removed from the afternoon teas that Mrs. Claymore had hosted.

Slade pointed toward the ground in front of the home. "I bet that's where they found Richard Claymore."

"Creeps me out," Larry said. "I feel sorry for Dickie. Poor kid just hangin' out and the whole family is killed by some psycho."

Wendy shivered.

"I saw him," Kevin announced.

The others looked at him.

"What are you talkin' about?" Larry asked. "Saw who?"

"Richard Claymore. Or his apparition. Or somethin'."

"His appa what?" Larry said.

Kevin stared at the house. "Apparition. That means his ghost."

"Wha . . . when?" Wendy asked.

Kevin turned his head toward the corner window and looked back at her. "That first day we came down here. When we were ridin' by. I looked up and the ghost was lookin' back."

"No way," Rut said. "Cool!"

"Bull crap, man. You didn't see anythin'," Slade said.

"I did too!" Kevin looked toward the house and pointed. "Right in that window. A man stared back at me. It had to be the ghost of Richard Claymore. What else could it be? And when we came by here real late the other night, a light came on. There's a ghost livin' there."

"Let's go in," Rut said.

"No way!" Wendy said.

"Why not?" Rut asked.

Wendy looked at him with disgust. "First of all, it's trespassin'. You know. Illegal. Second of all, it's haunted. I ain't goin' in no haunted house."

"I'll go!" Slade said.

"There's no way I'm goin' in there," Kevin said.

"I'm goin'." Slade laid his bike down.

Rut followed suit.

"You comin'?" Slade asked Larry.

Larry shrugged.

"Don't be a wuss," Slade said.

Larry pondered for a moment. "Okay, I'll go."

Slade led the way with Rut and Larry safely a half-step behind as they crossed the road.

Kevin and Wendy sat on their bikes next to the three lying on their side.

Wendy disapprovingly crossed her arms. "Idiots. I hope they get the crap scared out of 'em."

Kevin nodded. "You don't mess with ghosts. And who knows? Might be three ghosts. Mrs. Claymore and the sister too. They might just be waitin' for three idiots to come in there so they can scare the crap out of 'em."

"Look at 'em." Wendy chuckled. "They're takin' forever." She cupped her hands. "Hey, hurry up. We don't have all day."

Rut looked back and swatted his hand at her.

"This ain't good." Kevin shook his head. "Ain't good."

The closer they got, the more cautiously they walked.

Rut moved next to Larry, almost touching him.

"Y'all should hold hands," Wendy yelled.

They reached the first step. The porch had several holes large enough for a foot to go through.

Larry looked back at Kevin.

Kevin held up his hands with an "I don't know what to tell you" gesture.

Slade took the first step, skipped the second, and stood on the porch.

Rut and Larry took them one at a time.

Slade looked left and right down the porch. He made a fist and knocked on the door.

"Why did you knock?" Rut asked. "Do you think the ghost is gonna open it and say come on in?"

Slade shrugged. "I dunno."

Rut reached for the door knob and turned it slowly.

"What are you doin', Rut?" Larry asked.

Rut shrugged.

Click.

He pushed the door.

Creak.

It slowly opened.

A whiff of mustiness flowed out. Rut saw the bottom of the stairs leading to the second floor. The open door offered most of the light coming into the house.

Rut took a step toward the threshold.

The door swung back and closed.

Bang!

Rut fell down to his backside.

Slade jumped off the porch.

Rut scooted back.

Larry helped him up and they followed Slade, who'd already made it twenty yards from the house.

Kevin snickered and looked at Wendy. "Chickens."

Slade neared and shouted at Kevin and Wendy, "Runnnnn!"

Wendy looked at Kevin with eyes widened.

Teenagers have certain unwritten rules. One of those is that when one teen tells another to run, they run, no questions asked. They were on bikes, but they understood the universal cry of "run" just the same.

Dirt and gravel flew from their tires as the five barreled down Devil's Backbone toward the highway.

Kevin rode ten bike lengths ahead of the pack. He wouldn't be caught in the rear this time with the Claymore house staring back.

No one spoke as they pedaled with fury, struggling to avoid holes and fallen branches.

Kevin reached the parking lot of Pollard's Lumber and stopped.

Within seconds, all four reached him.

"What happened?" he asked.

Slade, out of breath, looked at Rut. "I knocked. Not sure why. Then Rut just opened the door. It opened real slow and creepy like. Then it shut."

Rut laid his head on his handlebars. "Man, that scared the crap out of me."

Wendy offered a skeptical tone. "Maybe the wind blew it closed. Ever think of that?"

"Bull crap!" Rut said. "Someone pushed it closed. It knocked me down."

"Not someone. Some thing," Kevin suggested.

"Well, serves you right for trespassin'," Wendy said.

"I ain't ever doin' that again," Larry said.

"I ain't goin' back by there," Rut said.

"What? What about the fort?" Slade asked.

Larry shook his head. "Nuh-uh. No way, I'm not goin' back. Not today anyways."

"Fine. I'm thirsty. Let's go over to DQ and at least get a drink or somethin'," Slade said.

CHAPTER 11

THEY SCRAPED TOGETHER enough change to buy two Cokes and share. They piled into a booth with Rut barely sitting on the edge of one side. The air conditioning cooled them off.

"I've never been so scared in my life," Rut said.

"Forget about it," Slade said. "Probably just the wind like Wendy said."

"No!" Kevin slapped the table. Realizing how loud he'd been, he lowered his head and his voice. "Are y'all forgettin'? Remember what I saw. It was the ghost of Richard Claymore. What else would it have been?"

"Your mind is playin' tricks on you?" Slade suggested. "There ain't no such thing as ghosts. It's like that story Wendy told. It wasn't no ghost. It was her mom."

"I believe in ghosts anyway," Wendy said.

"Me too," Rut offered. "What about you, Larry?"

He shrugged. "I don't know. Seems pretty crazy. But, if it's true, probably not just Richard Claymore's ghost. His wife and daughter too. The whole place is haunted."

Wendy dropped her mouth. "That's what Kevin just said to

me. Three ghosts."

"Y'all are crazy, man," Slade said.

Larry grinned. "All right, tough guy. How about we go back right now, and you go in by yourself, look around, see if anythin's there? If you stay in for five minutes and survive, we'll know there ain't no ghosts."

Wendy gave Slade the "I dare you" look.

"Man, I ain't ridin' all the way back there for that. Maybe some other time," Slade said.

"Uh-huh. That's what I thought." Larry crossed his arms.

Kevin looked over at a nearby table where three men in their seventies and eighties played cards—the DQ Bunch. "I bet they know somethin' about all this. Look how old they are. They probably lived here forever. Let's go ask 'em."

Rut looked over. "Not me. I ain't—"

Kevin exited the booth and walked the twelve feet slowly as cards slapped the table and the men yammered on about baseball statistics. He stopped at the edge as the four men stopped their game and looked up.

One of them laid down his hand of cards. He wore an orange ball cap with the Gulf Oil emblem. "Can we help you, son?"

Kevin swallowed. He turned and pointed in the direction of Devil's Backbone, far from sight. "Do y'all know anythin' about that Claymore mansion? We heard there was a murder there a long time ago."

One of them, who seemed to have more hair coming out of his ears than on his head, said, "What that young feller say?"

The one next to him leaned over. "Wants to know about the Claymore murders."

The man with the extra hairy ears nodded and leaned back.

"Yep. We know all about it. Pull up a chair and we'll tell you."

The one with the ball cap extended his hand. "I'm Bill. What's your name?"

"Kevin," he said with a curt nod.

The DQ Bunch relished the opportunity.

Kevin took the empty chair.

Bill noticed the other four kids staring. "Y'all might as well pull up a chair."

They quickly exited the booth and joined Kevin.

Bill did most of the talking as he recounted what they had learned from the newspaper articles. One of the other men would occasionally interrupt him to offer a brief anecdote or correction. Or someone would restate something to the man in desperate need of a hearing aid.

"You have to forgive ole Jesse," Bill said, thumbing at him. "Can hardly hear a damn thing. He's eighty-four years old. But his memory's as solid as they come. Hey, Jesse!" Bill spoke loud enough for everyone at Dairy Queen to hear, but no other patrons were there.

Jesse cupped his ear.

"Tell these kids about Richard Claymore," Bill said.

"Ah." Jesse cleared his throat and sipped his coffee. "Well, I knew Claymore pretty good. He hired me and another feller to do some work around the house now and then. His wife, Clara, was always wanting to change something up around there. Real pretty gal. Always gussied up with her hair and a fancy dress. Claymore was quite smitten with her. If she asked for something, she got it, within reason.

"When they first planned to build that mansion, it was gonna be thirty-something rooms. She settled on twenty-something. They moved in when it was only partially done. She would do one room up first class and move to the next. Used the outhouse until they had their fancy bathrooms put in. Each person even had their own bathroom. Can you imagine that?

"Didn't just have a kitchen but also had what you call a butler's pantry. Real fancy.

"Two little rugrat kids running around. Seemed kinda spoiled but not too bad. The little boy, Dickie, would ask to help so we'd give him something to do. He'd get good and dirty, and she'd fuss at him but then give us a wink.

"She'd have us repaint one of the outbuildings or tend her garden. She couldn't grow nothing, but we showed her when to plant. Kept the weeds and pests out. Seemed like a lot of useless work. We found out later, she heard we were out of work. And that was true. Times were tough back then to find work. I was barely out of school and my daddy didn't allow no loafing.

"One time she had four or five of us out there working. Seems like a couple of us would dig a hole and a couple of others would fill it in.

"So, yeah, I knew 'em pretty good, but a lot of others didn't like 'em. 'Cuz he was the DA. You know, the one that sends people off to the penitentiary. Well, him and the judge."

"Yeah, Jesse, we told them about Marshall Pollard and getting sent off," Bill said.

Jesse nodded. "Yep. Pollard was one. Also this older feller name of Samuel Crabtree. Was a Yankee soldier in the Civil War. Came from Ohio. Liked to get drunk and brag how he whooped the Rebels at Gettysburg. Not too popular a thing to say around these parts. Anyways, he got caught thieving a horse and Claymore was the prosecutor. Slam dunk. Everyone knew he was guilty. I was outside the courthouse when they took him off. Right before the murders, we heard he and a few others escaped from a chain gang. Thought he might've been the one that killed them but later learned he was caught a couple of weeks before.

"You see, with a job like Claymore had, any number of folks might want to see him dead."

Bill's unplayed hand remained on the table. He'd occasionally pick it up and shuffle. He threw the cards toward the center of the table.

He slid his chair toward them and continued, "For weeks and weeks, no one found any clues to the murder. No suspects. Nothing. At first, reporters from Houston and Dallas came around asking the same people the same questions. The sheriff called the Texas Rangers to come and investigate. They were in and out of that house a hundred times. Hired a bunch of men to go with them into the woods. Even had some trained dogs out there trying to find something.

"Then, the big city reporters showed up. One from New York came down. He's the one that wrote that detective all the way over in London that had worked on the Jack the Ripper case. Asked him to come investigate."

"The what?" Kevin asked.

"Jack the Ripper is a real famous case of this man that killed a bunch of women in London getting near on a hundred years ago. The case is still unsolved. This detective worked on that case and specialized in unsolved murders. I was your age back then, but I remember him. Real prim and proper. Had that British accent. Nice feller. Always rubbing his chin while he was thinking."

"There used to be a cafe downtown. We didn't have no Dairy Queen back then," Bill said with a smile. "He was here for near two weeks. Every evening, he'd have his supper in there. We'd wait for him to finish and ask him about the case.

"He'd walk out, light his pipe, and say, 'How are you chaps this fine evening?'" Bill failed at a British accent.

"One of us would ask, 'Have you solved the case, mister?'

"He'd say, 'Not yet, my good man, but I'm very close.'

"Well, he never solved it either, obviously. That's about it."

Jesse spoke up. "You told 'em about the British feller?"

Bill nodded. "Just did."

Jesse looked at the kids and continued, "Me and some of them other fellers that the Claymores had been so nice to fixed up the cemetery by their house and helped bury them. Dang near the whole town showed up. Awful sad time."

"Did any of you know Dickie?" Wendy asked.

"Why sure," Bill answered. "I s'pose we all knew him. But Frank, here, knew him the best."

Frank nodded. He'd kept quiet for the whole conversation with the teens and occasionally offered an approving nod. He wore overalls and rested his hands inside the buckled front. He lowered his head and grinned as he prepared his story.

"Well, Dickie and I were real good friends. We were about the same age as you. He went to school with all of us. Just had one schoolhouse back then and he was in my class. His momma also taught him and his sister a lot at home. Made them do extra work, so he was always ahead of us in his schoolin'. Taught 'em piano and French. When he had to go home, he'd say 'adieu,' which is French for goodbye. I tried to—"

"Paula, your order is ready!" A DQ worker blurted over the loudspeaker.

Frank looked over his shoulder, annoyed at the interruption. He looked back shaking his head. "Now, where was I? Oh, yeah. I tried to keep up with his learnin', but he sorta was better at everythin'. Real athletic too. We played a lotta baseball, and he was faster than anybody runnin' around the bases. We played a lot out in those woods around their house. A few boys from town would meet us. I lived a mile north of town, so my daddy would let me ride my horse, Trixie, out there.

"We played hide-and-seek, probably just like you kids. But we also played this game called ghost in the graveyard. Kinda backwards to hide-and-seek. One person is 'it' and he goes and hides. The rest of the players count from the base and then go out and find him. You have to play when it's dark, so it's good and scary. The one hidin' tries to jump out and scare them and then run to the base before they catch him."

Kevin turned to Larry and smiled at the idea of that game.

"Well, Dickie was better than any of us. He knew them woods like the back of his hand. Better than anybody. He always found the best hidin' spot and then knew some little trick or shortcut to get to base faster than we could catch him.

"Come to think of it, we was just like you kids. Dickie and some of us would go into Pollard's General Store. It's the hardware store now, but back then they sold all kinds of stuff. There'd be some old fellers sittin' in the corner playin' cards on top of a wooden barrel. We'd go listen to their war stories. See, these were Civil War veterans.

"I especially remember this one with a long gray beard." Frank stroked his chin.

"He smoked a pipe and folks called him Whistle 'cuz he sorta whistled when he talked. Dickie would ask him tons of questions about the war, and ole Whistle loved it. He especially liked talkin' about the First Battle of Manassas. Yankees called it Bull Run."

Frank paused for a moment as a DQ worker making a milkshake drowned them out with noise from the mixer.

"Some of the other kids teased Dickie, thinkin' he thought he was better than them. He was the only rich kid in town. Rest of us hardly had two nickels to rub together and only a couple sets of clothes. His momma made him dress real nice for school and extra fancy for church. He hated that and would get all dirty on purpose.

"One time, this mean kid we called Skipper really was givin' Dickie a hard time. He was two years older and obviously bigger. He was pushin' on Dickie behind the school where we played ball. Callin' him a momma's boy and fancy pants. Stuff like that. Pushed him real hard to the ground. Skipper was lookin' around and laughin'. But none of us were laughin'. We liked Dickie. And we hated Skipper. He was a bully. A couple of us helped him up, but when Dickie stood, he pushed us away. He put up his dukes."

Frank put his hands up in a boxing pose.

"'You want to fight? I'll whip you good,' Dickie said.

"Skipper just laughed at him. 'You think you can whoop me?'

"Before ya know it, Dickie punched him in the face three times real fast. Jabs with his left hand. Then Skipper was the one on his back side. Stunned. He hopped up and took a couple of swings at Dickie, but Dickie bobbed his head around. Then Dickie reared back with his right and whopped him in the cheek. A terrific blow. Skipper's head went to the side, and he fell down, unconscious. We just looked at him for a few seconds and then he opened his eyes. Shook his head and crawled up to his feet. Walked away rubbin' his jaw."

Slade pumped his fist in approval.

Rut nodded.

"We was pattin' Dickie on the back, but he wasn't smilin'. He just walked off. We found out later that his momma wasn't the only one teachin' Dickie things. Turns out his daddy knew a thing or two about boxin'. They had this bag they filled with hay and hung from a tree, and Dickie would practice punchin' it."

A bell on the door jingled as another DQ customer walked in.

"The last fun time we had together was right before the

murders. His parents threw him a party for his thirteenth birthday. They had all this fancy food and cake and punch. We played a bunch of games. His parents gave him this real nice kite and let all of us fly it.

"That was a real fun day. It was the day before the murders. I was the last one to leave. I was ridin' away on Trixie and looked back. Dickie was holdin' his kite. His daddy's hand was on Dickie's shoulder. His momma was holdin' her daughter's hand. They all waved goodbye to me. I waved back and said, 'Adieu.'"

Frank lowered his head. "Such a nice family. Happy family. Darn shame."

Wendy wiped tears from her eyes.

CHAPTER 12

A WOMAN WITH a young daughter and her daughter's three friends walked into Dairy Queen and ordered soft-serve ice cream on cones. They sat in the back, licking their tasty treats, and chatted.

Slade had stepped out to talk with two school friends that rode their bikes near DQ.

It was a typical summer day in Mead Creek, except that Kevin and his friends listened to stories that mesmerized them.

"Mrs. Oberlin over at the library told us about this sheriff that took Dickie in, and how Dickie went off to fight in World War I," Kevin said.

Bill nodded. "Yep."

Frank nodded as well. "That's about the size of it. Dickie kinda kept to himself. Never wanted to play ball or go out in the woods with us like he used to. He sorta remained in shock for years. Got to where he kept himself inside all the time. When America got involved in The Great War . . . y'all probably call it World War I," Frank said, looking down at the kids, "they was gonna start draftin' people. Dickie just ran off to Dallas and joined up.

"My daddy asked Sheriff Brown about it, but he just said they got a letter from Dickie that he was headed over to Europe. I got drafted and weren't too far behind. Next thing you know, I was in a trench waitin' for the whistle to blow for us to charge the Germans."

"Frank's getting a bit off track," Bill said. "We heard from some of the big city papers that Dickie was a hero in the war. Headlines like 'Son of slain family slays the Huns.'"

"Huns?" Rut asked.

"That's one of the names we had for Germans," Bill answered. "The papers said he was fighting in the Battle of the Argonne Forest. This whole bunch of American soldiers and Dickie were trapped by three German machine guns. Just a matter of time before they'd be totally surrounded and the Germans would move in and get 'em. Well, this was a new area of operation for the Germans, but Dickie knew it real good. Kinda like he knew those Mead Creek woods.

"Dickie took off, jumping around real sneaky and hiding behind trees. He got behind one German machine gun and shot 'em all. There was so much noise and confusion, none of the other Germans even saw Dickie. He took out the next machine gun squad, but the last one, and the one closest to the Americans, was across this open area.

"Dickie jumped in the Germans' trench and had to kill two or three of 'em with his bayonet. Then, he jumped out of the trench and threw a grenade at the last one. Papers said he killed nine Germans in about ten minutes. They gave him the Distinguished Service Cross. One of the highest awards you can get for bravery."

Frank snickered. "Well, that's pretty close, but Bill tells the story a little different each time. Point is, Dickie was a war hero."

Slade had walked back in to hear of Dickie's heroics. "Man, he was somethin' else."

"So, you were in the war with Dickie?" Larry asked Frank.

Frank chuckled. "Nah. There were thousands of us fightin'

over there. Most of us just came back home and went about our lives. Dickie shows up about two years after the rest of us. Sheriff Brown had passed, but his wife still lived there in town. I went over to the house, and Dickie came out to the porch. We talked for a bit, but he still had that look. Just like after his family was murdered. He just sorta looked past you. No emotion. He didn't really want to talk about the war or anythin'. Said that after the war ended, he just wandered around for a bit."

Frank shook his head, and no one spoke for a moment.

The teens looked at one another.

Frank spoke again. "Turns out, Dickie's father had set up a trust in case anythin' were to happen, and Sheriff Brown made sure it was all managed by some accountant in Dallas. Dickie's mom had a whole lot more money than any of us thought. A whole bunch just sittin' in the bank, drawin' interest. The house and land all paid for. So, Dickie didn't need to work or nothin'. But he stayed in town with Mrs. Brown and took care of her. But, like I said, just kept to himself, stayed inside and never married. One day—"

The noise of a large crowd entering Dairy Queen interrupted Frank. One boy pitched a baseball back and forth from his bare hand to a glove.

Larry elbowed Slade and nodded toward the clock on the wall. "We got a game!" Slade said. They both stood quickly. "Sorry. We gotta go."

"Yeah. Last game of the season," Rut said. "Thanks for the stories," he said to the elderly men.

Kevin and Wendy stood as well. "Thank you," she said.

Bill lightly grabbed Kevin's arm. "You ever hear of a book called *In Cold Blood* by Truman Capote?"

Kevin shook his head.

"You might find it interesting."

As Kevin walked out the door, Jesse leaned over to Bill and said, "Y'all tell 'em about Dickie still living in that old mansion?"

Bill shook his head. "I was about to, but they done run off. Guess they'll figure it out sometime."

———————— •◉• ————————

SLADE, LARRY, AND Rut rode their bikes at high speed toward home to prepare for their baseball games.

Wendy and Kevin took it much slower, discussing all they heard from the DQ Bunch. They headed for the library.

Once inside, they noticed Mrs. Oberlin busy with other patrons. They looked through several drawers and argued back and forth over the title and name of the author.

"Here it is!" Wendy said. "364.1 Ca."

"What does that mean?" Kevin asked.

Wendy shrugged. "Think that means where we find it. Kinda wish I'd paid more attention when we were learnin' that Dewey Decimal stuff."

They walked up and down several aisles before noticing one that had "C-D" on an end-cap sign. They found dozens of books with authors whose last names started with "C" and that had 364 on the library label.

"Found it!" Kevin announced.

The copy's brown cover had an impersonal, protective, plastic wrapping. Kevin tucked it under his arm. "Let's go."

They walked toward the door.

"Eh-hum."

They turned to find Mrs. Oberlin with her arms crossed. "Forgetting something?"

Kevin and Wendy widened their eyes, realizing they hadn't checked the book out.

Mrs. Oberlin smiled and curled her finger. "C'mon. Let's get you checked out."

Behind the counter, she filled out a card and handed the book back to Kevin. "This is a very serious book, but it's a classic. Let me guess, your interest in this is similar to your interest in the Claymore murders, isn't it?"

Kevin shrugged. "Somebody just said we'd like to read it. Is it about the Claymore murders?"

"No. But it's similar. It's about a farm family murdered in Kansas twenty years ago. I'd love to say enjoy it, but it's a pretty dark subject."

They left with their now-legally-checked-out book and sat on the front steps. The book's spine had "*In Cold Blood* by Truman Capote," but Kevin rubbed his finger over the large T and C of the author's initials on the front cover. He opened to the first few pages. "A true account of a multiple murder and its consequences." He looked at Wendy with an open mouth and flipped to another page.

She reached for the book and read. "'For Jack Dunphy and Harper Lee with my love and gratitude.' I wonder who that is."

Kevin shrugged as she flipped several pages. She read two excerpts. "'Girl shot in the back of the head . . . blood covered the walls.' Dang. This is just like the Claymore murders."

"I'm gonna read this startin' tonight," Kevin said.

She closed the book and handed it back to him. "Okay. But I want it when you're done." She stood and brushed off her backside.

Kevin looked up at her with a blank stare. Wendy wasn't a tomboy, but she had no problem getting dirty and building a fort. Kevin had always liked spending time with her. But ever since they started their daily treks to the fort, his admiration of her spunkiness had turned into appreciation for her beauty. Some might say he was smitten. Maybe not deep, head-over-heels, in love. His peers would say he "liked" her.

"What are you lookin' at?" she asked with a smile.

He shook his head. "Oh . . . nothin'."

CHAPTER 13

"THE TELEPHONE IS ringing. You got me on the run." Alice Cooper's "Under My Wheels" blared over the large box speakers hanging from two corners at The Oz Arcade. The local youth frequented the establishment to play rows of pinball machines and spin kicks on the foosball table, while some older teens played pool for dollar bets.

The arcade was named for Oz and Lydia Cohn, who had escaped Nazi Germany in 1938 for opportunities in New York. Dissatisfied with big city life, they moved south to a small town at the suggestion of friends. They opened a map, pointed, and left their fate in the hands of Mead Creek, Texas. With barely $200, they arrived by bus with two young children, three suitcases, and promises of the American dream.

Lydia took in sewing, and Oz hired himself out fixing appliances with skills he'd learned in his father's blacksmith shop. After selling used washers and refrigerators he'd repaired out of a rented barn, Oz leased retail space in 1961 and opened Mead Creek's first appliance store. Within the next few years, he also opened a laundromat and a tailor shop run by Lydia. Oz eventually bought the downtown building, which housed seven retail spots. The renter had become the landlord.

After the sheriff complained of some local teen mischief, Oz's entrepreneurial side sparked an idea for one of his empty locations, and he started the town's first and only arcade. Some locals frowned upon the idea of teens gathering and the potential for trouble, but Oz and Lydia enjoyed the youthful crowd now that their two children had grown and moved away.

Oz hated the rock music his customers craved, but he knew it was good for business to keep the radio on KPRW, Power FM 89.7. Most Mead Creek teens set their clock radio alarms to wake them with music from that station.

A deep, bass voice talked over the song as it wound down. "You've got John 'The Rock' Rolls playing your power hits on this scorcher of a day. Temperature's gonna reach 101 today, so stay cool, as we've got Journey, E.L.O., and Supertramp coming. Right now, here's Van Halen and 'D.O.A.'"

A slender teen threw back his long, blond locks and mimicked Eddie Van Halen's riffs on his air guitar.

Aside from the music, games, and cold beverages from the Coke machine, teens found The Oz, as they called it, a fun place to hang out because it was a no-parents zone. Before the arcade opened, kids took turns on three pinball machines at the eight-lane bowling alley or on the gunfight game at Piggly Wiggly. Aside from Oz, and the sheriff, who performed the occasional walk-thru, adults never ventured inside.

Slade banged on the most popular video game in the arcade—*Space Invaders*. He rotated his hips in movement with the game. Some players had learned the sequencing to achieve advancement and high scores by timing their shots. Slade currently owned the number two spot on the highest scores, behind someone with the initials HEB.

No one played the game to the left—*Breakout*, or the game on the right—*Night Driver*.

Slade chewed on a straw and wore no shirt, having tucked it in the back pocket of his cutoffs for no particular reason. Like most, he had developed a deep tan at this point in the summer from daily swimming.

Ironically, the sign that said NO SHIRT, NO SHOES, NO SERVICE hung just over the *Space Invaders* game, but Oz rarely enforced his own rules. Not the petty ones anyway. However, he didn't tolerate drugs, alcohol, or fighting. He may have been nearing seventy, but he'd grabbed more than one violator by the shirttail and threw them out.

"Don't come back for a week" was his usual punishment. Teens found his German accent authoritative although a few equated him to Sergeant Schultz from *Hogan's Heroes*.

Unlike getting in trouble with a teacher, the sheriff, or your parents, it was uncool to get punished by Oz. A week later, he typically welcomed the wayward teen back with open arms.

Larry and Kevin stood on either side of Slade. Two weeks had passed since their scare at the Claymore mansion and tales of the young Dickie Claymore that witnessed it all. None of them had suggested a return to the fort, or the Creek, as their secret code required it be called. Slade's parents sent him to his grandparents in West Texas for a week. Wendy and Rut had supposedly just returned from their family's summer vacation.

"Man. Right there. You're gonna miss it," Larry barked at Slade.

"I know what I'm doin'," Slade said. "You know whose initials are number two on this game?"

Revvvv! Revvvv!

Everyone in the arcade turned their heads toward the front

section of the arcade, looking through glass that was from floor to ceiling.

The 1969 Chevy Chevelle SS had one red racing stripe that ran the length of each side while the remainder of the car glistened in black. The sun beamed off the hood. Everyone knew the car and that it had a 396-inch Big-Block engine with a four-barrel carburetor, as its driver, Wayne Moretti, reminded anyone who even looked at it. Few knew what that meant, or whether it made his car fast. But they knew it sounded cool when he said it, and it sounded even cooler when he started it.

Slade had turned back to his game, but Larry and Kevin followed Wayne's entrance into the arcade, careful not to make direct eye contact.

Kevin said a little prayer that he wouldn't want to play *Space Invaders* and force Slade into giving up on his game.

Wayne Moretti wasn't the town bully, but his reputation suggested that he feared no man. Kevin had heard several myths surrounding his legendary status. Although a high school junior, he looked as though he should have graduated years ago. He lived with his mother a quarter mile out of town. His father was absent from the home, rumored to be a prison guard at Huntsville and responsible for Moretti's demeanor.

Moretti wore his curly hair past his collar and parted in the middle. His upper lip sported a thin mustache with accompanying stubble on his chin. As he walked by Kevin and Larry, and they exhaled, Moretti brushed through his locks and returned the comb to his back pocket. While everyone else wore shorts, he wore jeans and a Bad Company concert T-shirt. He walked with confidence. Stories about him always had some element of "he doesn't start a fight, but he'll sure finish one."

He headed for the pool tables in the back as a couple of high schoolers lifted their heads to say hello.

The back of the arcade housed two pool tables and represented a sort of no man's land for the middle school teens. If high schoolers were playing, all others stayed clear.

Kevin looked over the young men throughout the establishment and wondered if one of them might be stupid enough to tangle with Wayne Moretti, the toughest kid in Mead Creek.

"Crap!" Slade shouted, as his game ended nowhere near his record.

Larry inserted a quarter in the slot. "My turn, turd face. Step back and let me show you how it's done."

"When are Rut and his pain-in-the-butt sister comin' home?" Slade asked.

Kevin shrugged. "Pretty soon, I guess."

"They got back last night," Larry said. "Saw 'em when we were drivin' by and they were unloadin' their car."

Kevin hadn't seen Wendy since their ride home from the library two weeks prior. He'd thought about her every day. He'd never gone steady with a girl. Lori Sparks told everyone they were "going together" last semester, but Kevin told everyone he never officially agreed. He once made out with Wendy Patsone at a party at Slade's house in sixth grade, but their relationship never materialized. Kevin had liked other girls, but his affections for Wendy were something he'd never felt before.

Kevin looked toward the door. "Hey, there's their mom's car."

Rut hopped out of one side and Wendy out of the other. Their mom yelled something, and Wendy nodded back as they entered the arcade.

Rut walked up to Slade for a gimme-five slap and offered the same to Kevin. "Can I play next?" Rut asked Larry.

As Wendy approached, Kevin smiled and said, "Hey, Wendy!"

She looked down with her arms crossed. She barely lifted her head to acknowledge him.

Kevin noticed the tears welled up in her eyes. He turned and watched her as she joined two other girls she knew from school by an old, rarely played, Elvis-themed pinball machine.

Kevin lightly backhanded Rut on the arm. "What's wrong with your sister?"

Rut looked toward her and back at Kevin. "Remember how I said my parents were gettin' a divorce, and she said they weren't?"

Kevin nodded.

"Well, after we got home from our vacation, my dad said he wasn't unpackin' and is movin' out. Movin' all the way to Dallas for some new job. It was decided several weeks ago, but they didn't wanna spoil our vacation. My mom said they're just separatin' and that it doesn't mean they're gettin' a divorce, but parents always say that." Rut looked at Wendy again. "She's takin' it pretty hard. Guess I knew it was gonna happen eventually." Rut shrugged.

Kevin had never seen Rut look at his sister with anything but contempt. Now, he looked at her with compassion.

"Dang, man, that sucks. Sorry," Larry said, without turning from the game.

Slade put his hand on Rut's shoulder. "Yeah, man. Sorry."

Rut acknowledged with a slight head lift and tuned in to Larry's progress on *Space Invaders*. Enemy ships had killed him twice, and he only had one life left.

Kevin slow-walked toward Wendy, searching for words that might comfort her.

As he approached, all three girls looked back at him.

He knew all of them, and, on any given day, would fear a one-on-one conversation with any of them. Holding court with three older girls at the same time was Slade's territory. He opened his mouth, but no words came out.

Wendy saved him with a "Hey, Kevin" that broke the ice. She wiped her eyes.

One of the two other girls gave a curt wave.

"Hey. Rut just told us about your parents. So sorry."

She brushed her hair behind her ear, frowned, and sniffed. "Thanks." She grabbed his wrist and pulled him in between an Elvis-themed pinball machine and another with no real theme other than big-breasted women.

The other girls turned toward the older boys playing pool.

"I really never thought this would happen. I knew they had problems and argued a bunch, but don't all parents do that?" She folded her arms and shook her head.

A slight guilt overcame Kevin. He knew that his job, at that moment, was to be a good friend to Wendy. To listen and console. However, he couldn't help but relish that grab of the wrist and her request to be alone with him—even in an arcade full of kids with games pinging, cracking, and jingling. He looked in her eyes and nodded.

She continued, "I asked my dad, I mean, begged him, to just stay. That I'd talk to mom and get her to chill out about everythin'. But, he wouldn't listen. Said it was no use. Said she won't change. Said he tried to meet her more than halfway more than once."

"What about talkin' to your mom?" Kevin asked.

She scoffed. "Ha. No way. She's so set in her ways. Thinks she knows everythin'. She keeps our furniture and carpet covered with plastic. Can't touch anythin'. Strict curfew. Always tellin' me what I can and can't wear. Not real flexible, ya know. I mean, she's not evil. But she sure don't care what nobody else thinks. I may just move out with my dad."

Kevin's eyes widened. "No! I mean . . . you don't wanna do

that. What about leavin' Rut all alone? What about your friends? And school?" Kevin immediately regretted his words, realizing he selfishly wanted her to stay. He reversed himself with some nonsensical advice. "I just mean unless you think that's better."

She tapped on the pinball machine glass and looked up at Elvis's white suit. "I know. I don't want to leave Mead Creek. Don't wanna have to make new friends. Besides, Dallas is only a couple hours away. He said we could go there some weekends and some weekends he'd come here. Guess it won't be all bad."

"Yeah, that's right. It won't be that bad," he said with a grin.

She smiled and reached out to hug him.

He hugged back, satisfied that he'd resolved her problem, and relieved that she put away notions of moving to Dallas. He wanted the hug to last forever.

As if on cue, Journey began playing over the radio.

They released and both stood there awkwardly, as he was blocking her path out between the two pinball machines.

"You gonna let me out?" she said.

He laughed and backed out without looking. He stepped on a foot and ran into another body. A cold liquid ran down his back and he heard the nearly full can hit the floor. Kevin turned as Wayne Moretti looked back.

Dr. Pepper trickled out of the can and ran between Kevin's feet.

Kevin was thankful that he had just used the restroom and emptied his bladder. The teeth chattering began with his molars and progressed toward his incisors.

Although a recent growth spurt gave Kevin two inches above his peers, Moretti towered over him. In reality, Moretti was short for his age and only a head taller than Kevin. Moretti's left fist opened and closed.

The crushing sound from Larry's *Space Invaders* game ending, filled the arcade with an ironic tone.

Rut had alerted Slade and Larry to the unfolding event, and they turned to look.

Wendy remained in between the two pinball machines.

One by one, teens elbowed each other, and they turned from their games and conversations to the Moretti–Kevin standoff. A potential fight always outweighed entertainment from the twenty-five cents spent on an arcade game. A few souls inched closer to the altercation.

Those two pinball machines stood at the end of a long row ending near two pool tables. Girls could hang out there, but Kevin had operated dangerously close to no man's land.

Kevin swallowed. "Uh" was the best response he had to offer.

Moretti replied in a deep voice. "Uh. Is that all you've got to say?"

"Uh . . . sorry," Kevin murmured.

"You got any money?" Moretti asked.

That's it, Kevin thought. I can buy my way out of this situation.

At least Moretti would spare him from bodily harm and humiliation. He had two dollars in his pocket and some change. His friends could lend him more if needed.

"Uh . . . yeah. I've got like three bucks. But, I can get more. Way more. How much?"

Moretti cocked his head. "Three bucks? No, fifty cents. You knocked my Dr. Pepper out of my hands. I figure you owe me fifty cents."

Kevin, confused, reached into his pocket and sifted through some change. He held out his open hand full of change.

Moretti fingered through it, pulled out two quarters, and closed his fist around them. "Might want to look where you're going from now on." He turned and headed for the vending machines.

Kevin sighed.

Wendy worked her way from between the pinball machines and patted him on the shoulder. "Close one. You okay?"

Kevin bordered between shock and relief but was careful not to show weakness before the potential love of his life. "I'm cool," he said.

The ever-watchful Oz approached and plopped down a wet mop. "I'm happy you are cool. I would be cool with you cleaning my floor," he said.

"Yes, sir."

Kevin finished cleaning, tossed the nearly empty can in the trash, and returned the mop to a storage room next to the restrooms. He briskly walked through no man's land.

Moretti looked at him as he drank from his new Dr. Pepper.

When Kevin returned to the *Space Invaders* game, Rut had started on his turn.

"Man, we thought you were dead meat," Slade said.

Kevin exhaled.

Larry shook his head. "Man, I thought he was gonna take your head off."

"Don't worry. We would've jumped in and helped," Slade said.

"Pffft," Rut said, without turning from his game. "No way I would. That guy'll kill ya."

Slade punched Rut's arm. "Ow! You're gonna make me mess up." Rut stayed focused on his game.

"You gotta stick up for your friends. You better help if we ever need it," Slade said.

"I was just jokin'." He lifted his foot, rotated his hip, and tapped the laser button as fast and hard as he could.

"When are we goin' to the fo . . . uh . . . I mean the Creek again?" Larry said. "Let's go tomorrow. We haven't even talked about all that Claymore murder stuff."

"Cool with me," Rut said.

"Me too," Kevin said.

"Sure. I'm fixin' to leave. *Charlie's Angels* rerun and TV dinners tonight," Slade said.

Larry cocked his head. "You like that stupid show?"

Slade grinned. "I like lookin' at that show," he said, slowly. "Besides, it's good father–son bondin' time. Solvin' crimes with those ladies and eatin' Hungry-Man when my mom's at her bridge club." He walked away, putting his shirt on. "Later, losers."

"I'll go tell Wendy," Kevin said.

"Watch your step," Rut said, with a chuckle.

"Ha, ha." Kevin walked away thinking Rut had actually given sound advice. He made sure Wayne Moretti occupied himself far from Wendy and her companions.

Wendy leaned on the Elvis pinball machine with her back to Kevin.

One of the girls looked at Slade walking out. "Dang, that Slade's cute."

The other girl giggled.

Wendy looked over her shoulder in Slade's direction. Her mouth curled into a smile. "Yes, he is. He drives me crazy sometimes, but I think I like him."lace

Kevin paused. The girls had not noticed him approach. He backed away.

The news crushed him. It didn't shock him that other girls, even older girls, found Slade cute. He'd never been jealous of that before. A little envious, maybe. But not jealous. Until now.

Kevin returned to his friends.

"You tell her?" Larry asked.

Kevin looked down. "Uh, no. They were talkin'. Didn't want

to interrupt."

"All right. Make sure and tell her, Rut," Larry said.

"Yeah, yeah," Rut answered, focused on one of his best-ever performances on *Space Invaders*.

Kevin looked at Wendy, ignoring everything else.

CHAPTER 14

A
S THEY HAD done many times before, they rode past the Claymore mansion. No one suggested they stop and ponder the home, and none of them did. They barreled past it without looking.

The fort sat silent after no visits in the last two weeks. They left the door ajar and opened their makeshift window to allow the slight breeze to blow in. All five took their normal spots.

"Phew! Dang, it's hot in here." Rut fanned himself with his ball cap.

"Yep. Called Time and Temperature right before we left." Slade mimicked the auto-attendant. "Today's high: one-o-one. Current National Bank time: nine fifty-two. Temperature: ninety-one."

Wendy also mimicked a portion of the auto-attendant.

"We might need to jump in the creek and cool off, or we'll do that spontaneous combustion thing," Rut said.

"The what thing?" Larry asked.

"You know. Where you just go poof into nothin'." Rut made an exploding motion by opening his hands. "Poof!"

"That's horse crap. No way," Larry said.

"No, I heard about this," Slade said. "My dad said some guy

at work had it happen to his cousin."

"Oh, well. Must be true then," Larry said. "If your dad's cousin's mother's maid said it happened to their dog, must be true."

They all laughed.

Rut proudly wore his Cardinals ball cap. His team had won his league's championship, and he wasn't shy about bringing it up. "Should've brought my trophy out here but not sure it would fit in the fort. Too big."

"Oh, please," Slade said. "Who cares? Not like you did much to win."

"Excuse me! Catcher! Got a hit in the championship game too. Dang near made all-stars," Rut said.

Slade cocked his head. "But, you didn't, did ya?"

Kevin glanced at Wendy and wondered what she was thinking. How much did she like Slade? He glanced at Slade and slightly shook his head. He doesn't even know. Or care, he thought.

"Did you finish?" Wendy asked Kevin.

He didn't realize she was talking to him.

She lightly backslapped his arm. "Hey. Did you finish that book?"

"Oh, yeah. Read it all in, like, a week."

"What book?" Larry asked.

Everyone quieted for Kevin's response. "*In Cold Blood* by Truman Capote. One of those old guys at Dairy Queen said we should read it. It's about these two criminals who went to rob this farmer in Kansas. Broke in in the middle of the night while they were sleeping. They thought there was this safe with a whole lotta money. They couldn't find the money and woke up the family. Killed all of 'em, includin' kids."

"Just like the Claymore murders," Wendy said.

Kevin nodded. "Except they didn't leave no survivors. The

police caught 'em about a month later. They were hanged about fifteen years ago." Kevin held up his fist, holding a make-believe noose, cocked his head, and stuck his tongue out in mock execution.

"So, there's two big differences between that and the Claymore murders. Not only is Dickie an eyewitness, but the killer—" Kevin looked left and right at each of them for effect. "—is still out there."

"Yeah, but it was like sixty-five years ago. The killer's probably dead by now. Or caught for somethin' else and executed," Larry said.

Kevin folded his arms. "Maybe. But maybe not. Even so, we should try and solve this case."

"What for?" Rut asked.

Wendy smiled. "Oh, yeah. Might be fun. We can do our own investigation."

Kevin smiled at having pleased her.

Slade scoffed. "All right, Nancy Drew and Hardy Boy. You heard the guys at DQ. The sheriff, Texas Rangers, even that Scotland Yard detective couldn't solve it. What makes you think we can?"

"It's a cold case," Kevin said.

"A what?" Rut asked.

Kevin looked at him. "A cold case. I read about it in one of my dad's magazines. After a crime goes unsolved for a long time, they call it a cold case. Some detectives go back and try to solve the crime with new techniques and stuff. We need to look at this from a whole new, fresh perspective.

"We need to find out if there's any evidence to inspect or witnesses still alive that might know somethin'. And, we have to start with goin' to the scene of the crime."

Kevin couldn't believe the words that had come out of his mouth. He feared that house more than any of them. Its unseen dangers. The ghosts. The mysterious light coming on. The door slamming on Rut. A house dead on the outside but seemingly alive on the inside. But his inquisitive nature fueled his desire to investigate the crime. That, and Wendy's interest in solving the crime gave him all the motivation he needed.

Rut leaned toward Kevin. "Are you crazy? There's no way we're goin' back to that house. You wanna get killed by a ghost or whatever's hauntin' that place?"

"Screwwww that!" Slade said.

Larry remained silent and slightly shook his head.

Their strong reaction gave Kevin doubts.

Wendy brought him back. "I wanna see for myself. I don't think there's a ghost there. Just the wind or somethin' blew the door closed."

Rut swatted at his sister. "Fine. You and Detective Kevin can go have a tea party in there. But, I bet y'all come runnin' out of there in, like, twenty seconds."

"Yeah." Slade chuckled. "We'll stand guard . . . from like a mile away."

"Weren't you just givin' Rut a lecture about stickin' up for your friends?" Kevin asked Slade.

"Man, that's different. At least I can see who I'm fightin'. Ain't no tellin' what's in that house. Screw that."

Kevin stood and nearly hit his head on the low roof. He held out his hands. "We've got to solve this. For Dickie Claymore and his family. Think about his little sister. Same age as my little cousin." He pointed at Larry. "You always say the police think some other car ran your parents off the road and killed them. Maybe a drunk driver. Wouldn't you want to find out who did it?"

Larry shrugged. "Maybe."

Kevin turned to Slade. "You're always talkin' about your big sisters and how you would protect them if they ever needed it.

Don't you guys see? This is our chance to do somethin' good. Think about it. If we solved this, we'd be famous." He saw four blank stares. Even Wendy looked at Kevin with hesitation.

She broke the ice. "I'm in. Let's do it. Let's go to the house, right now."

"All right, all right," Slade said. "We'll do what y'all did. We'll stay by the road, and y'all can go in the house."

Rut and Larry nodded.

"It's decided then." He sat and pointed at the floor. "This will be like the police station. Any information we find, we keep here. We'll start with investigatin' the scene. We might need to ask those guys at Dairy Queen if they know anyone who was a witness."

"But, nobody was a witness except Dickie," Larry said.

Kevin looked at him. "Yeah, I know. I mean other people. Anyone the sheriff interviewed. Like did anyone see a stranger in town around that time? Or did anyone see someone ridin' out of town real fast? Stuff like that.

"And we have to figure out a motive. Who wanted to kill them? Nothin' was stolen, so it probably wasn't a robbery. Some guy with a grudge."

"Guys," Wendy said. "Remember, the newspaper said that Dickie saw three figures run away."

"That's right!" Kevin held up a finger. "That's the kind of detail we need to write down. We need to draw a diagram of what happened and a timeline. Make lists of everythin'."

"How do you know so much about this stuff?" Slade asked.

Kevin shrugged. "I dunno. You know. Books. Magazines. TV and stuff."

Rut chuckled. "Yeah, Slade. You watch *Charlie's Angels* all the time. You should be an expert at all this detective stuff."

Slade shot back at Rut. "I'm sure you don't ever miss a

Scooby-Doo on Saturday mornin'. You should be an expert on solvin' crimes."

"Yeah! We'll catch the bad guy and he'll say, 'I'd have gotten away with it, if it weren't for you meddlin' kids,'" Larry said.

The others shared in the laugh.

KEVIN LOOKED OVER his shoulder at Larry, Slade, and Rut sitting on their bikes across the Devil's Backbone road.

Rut leaned over to Slade and whispered out of Kevin's earshot. They both snickered.

Larry looked at Kevin and offered a salute as if to say, "Nice knowin' ya."

Kevin licked his lips. He stepped over an enormous ant pile. The front lawn of the Claymore mansion consisted of patches of weeds, dirt spots, and huge cracks in the earth from the lack of rain. He looked up at the sun with his left eye closed and the right squinted.

Wendy joined him on this adventure. They moved slowly.

He always appreciated time with her, but he thought Slade would make a better sidekick for this mission. Still, she braved this experience with him. The closer they got to the house, the closer they moved to one another.

At the bottom step of the front porch, her arm rubbed against his.

Kevin placed his arm across her front, blocking her from moving forward. "Maybe we should walk around and check out the back. See if there's a better place to go in."

She nodded.

They measured their steps carefully. Trees shaded the left side of the home and gave them slight relief from the scorching sun.

Wendy pointed up at two windows and whispered, "Wonder if that was the little girl's bedroom."

Kevin nodded, slowly.

They reached the back and discovered two more buildings that couldn't be seen from the road. A small barn and an outhouse. On any other day, an outhouse would cue a joke or some other type of bathroom humor. But not today.

A porch ran the length of the back of the house. A few pieces of screen clung to wood edges, and the porch appeared, at one time, to have been screened in.

Kevin elbowed Wendy. "Back door is wide open."

"Let's check out that side first," Wendy said.

The side facing the garage looked much like the other and offered no information or entrance.

"Let's—" Kevin paused. "I guess we don't need to whisper any. Not like anybody's here."

Slade saw them and yelled, "What are y'all doin'?"

Kevin swatted at him.

"Well. Guess we better go in," Wendy said.

Kevin nodded. He'd stalled long enough. His body tightened as they moved.

They walked around to the back and stepped onto the porch. A chair lay on its side next to a table and three other chairs. A shelf held dozens of old cans and bottles. A white deep freezer sat at the end with its chrome parts rusted.

They stopped at the threshold.

Wendy clutched Kevin's elbow.

His teeth began to chatter but he forced them to stop and swallowed hard.

They stepped in and looked left and right. Once inside, it seemed as if they'd stepped back in time. The open door and windows high in the front foyer let in sufficient light for them to make their way down a short hall along the staircase.

Kevin pointed to the floor and resumed whispering. "That might be where the mom was found."

The door on the left was closed, but to the right, a black stove sat in the middle of a kitchen beside two more closed doors.

Wendy slow-nodded as she examined the walls. She continued to grab his arm and then began to sing, quietly. "I lost myself in a familiar song. I closed my eyes, and I slipped away."

"What are you singin'?" he asked.

"Boston. 'More Than a Feeling.' It's what I sing when I'm nervous."

They sang together. "It's more than a feeling . . . more than a feeling."

They reached the bottom of the stairs, and to the right, they noticed books through a partially open door. Kevin pushed on the door, but rather than open toward the room, the pocket door slid into the wall. The office contained shelves of books from floor to ceiling. A giant, mahogany desk with intricate inlays sat in the middle of the room. A layer of dust covered more books stacked three and four high on the desk. On the wall, a portrait of a distinguished older gentleman in uniform looked back. The eyes followed them as they walked by. A huge globe rested on a stand and spindle in the corner.

Kevin imagined a thirteen-year-old Dickie spinning the globe and wondering about traveling to faraway places.

Kevin sniffed and didn't like it. That musty smell of old things. His parents liked one particular barbeque restaurant with antiques hanging from the wall. The smell usually made him lose his appetite.

On the other side, the parlor had a couch and two large chairs.

Kevin and Wendy leaned in and looked over the room. Intricate white paneling and gold trinkets gave the room a theme of elegance.

"No TV," Kevin said, in a feeble attempt at humor.

Wendy offered a smile that only made one side of her mouth curl up.

"Well, guess we should go check out the upstairs," she said.

Each step up the stairs had its own unique creak. They stopped a third of the way at a painting.

"That must be them," Kevin said.

The portrait showed a handsome family although none of them smiled. The Claymore father and son wore suits, and the mother and daughter wore light-colored dresses that covered every inch of skin aside from their hands and faces. Mr. Claymore, who looked to be in command, sported a handlebar mustache. Mrs. Claymore had high cheekbones and a refined appearance. Dickie showed poor posture, likely ready to change out of that suit and seek adventure in the woods.

Wendy blew on the painting to free it from dust.

Kevin coughed.

"Look at Ruth's hair," Wendy said. "Looks like it was blonde maybe and really curly. Cute girl."

Kevin nodded. "C'mon."

They found eight closed doors at the top of the stairs, and Kevin opened the first one to the left. A huge bed with corner posts that were six feet tall filled the room. Its linens were tightly tucked. The dresser held envelopes, a hairbrush, and a lady's hat on a small stand. A large book sat atop a slanted table whose only function seemed to be to exhibit the book.

Wendy mouthed the words "Holy Bible" on the book and noticed it open to the book of John.

Kevin reached for the door knob in an effort to hurry the

process. Although it was unspoken, they both wanted to make this investigative trip a quick one. That had been the room at the front of the house where a ghost had stared back at Kevin. He glared at the window where the ghost had hovered on that first day of summer. Spine-tingling fear ran through his body. He knew that another ghost might pop out at any moment, but protecting Wendy empowered him.

On the way to the next closed door, they saw that an open door revealed a bathroom.

"Two toilets?" Wendy asked.

Kevin shrugged.

One toilet had a ceramic tank overhead and a tin tank hovered over the shower. The sink and clawfoot tub completed the room.

The next door opened to a bedroom at the back of the house. Like the last room, it also had a bed, dresser, and hairbrush. However, these belonged to a little girl. A large doll lay on the pillow, and several others leaned or lay about the room.

"This is where they found her in the pink dress. Maybe right there or there." He pointed to each corner of the room. "Let's check for bloodstains." He knelt down on one side of the bed, but only a little light shone in through the drapes.

Wendy stroked the hair of a doll, its eyes glazed over with dust. The doll's white dress was yellow-stained on its edges.

Kevin inspected the other side of the bed thinking it might be where they found her body. Though brighter, this corner was still somewhat dark, so he reached for the drape to hold it back and let in some light. Indeed, several planks of the wood floor were stained. "This is it."

Wendy shook her head in disbelief. "So sad."

As Kevin prepared to release the drape, he looked toward one of the rear outbuildings. The same face that had stared at him from the Claymore mansion window now stared at him from beside the building.

Kevin's eyes widened. He felt trapped. He wanted to scream.

The figure had long white hair and a beard. It wore short-sleeved beige coveralls. In its right hand, a butcher knife glistened in the afternoon sun.

CHAPTER 15

K EVIN GRABBED WENDY'S wrist and pulled her out of the
room. "C'mon!"

"What?" She had no choice but to follow as Kevin maintained a tight grip.

They took the steps quickly as the staircase wound to a half-circle shape.

Kevin looked over his shoulder toward the back door where they had entered. He reached for the front door knob. His hand slipped off the handle as it failed to turn the lock. He pulled his hand from Wendy's wrist and used both hands to turn the knob.

"What is it? What happened?" she asked.

He glanced at her with fear in his eyes. "I saw somethin'. Out the window. A . . . a . . . somethin'. With a knife."

Her eyes widened. She noticed his failure to pull the door open. A metal cylinder with an oval handle stuck out above the knob. "A key!" she said. Wendy grasped the turn-of-the-century key and rotated it to the right.

Click!

Kevin turned the knob again, and the door opened.

They ran across the front porch, leaped over the steps, and

dashed toward their friends sitting on bikes.

Unlike the previous episode where Kevin and Wendy watched the other three run from the house, called them "chickens," and waited, Rut, Slade, and Larry immediately pedaled away.

Wendy and Kevin reached their bikes and followed, forty yards behind.

Gripped with fear, they darted away believing everything they'd ever heard about Devil's Backbone.

Kevin brought up the rear but didn't look back.

At the Claymore mansion, Dickie Claymore walked around the side of the house to the front and watched Kevin ride out of view. He shook his head, turned, and headed around to the back. His knife dripped with blood.

* ◆ *

THE TEENS HAD missed several things in their frequent trips by the Claymore estate. They never noticed the tire tracks leading to the unattached garage. They seemed to miss clothes hanging from a clothesline or the vegetable garden with several plants in rows. Boards and nails had been added to their fort for reinforcement without their notice.

During their walk around back, and then inside, Kevin and Wendy missed the trail leading to the outhouse. They failed to see a crossbow leaning against the back of the house. The freezer on the back porch buzzed. Present-day cans and food products were stacked on the kitchen counter. The home wasn't in near the state of disrepair that they thought. Their belief in an abandoned and possibly haunted house blinded them from the clues that a human being occupied the home.

As Kevin had looked at the figure from the window, he never considered that it might be Dickie Claymore. He only saw a scary-looking figure with a knife. He didn't see the butchered pig hanging from a tree with a broken arrow sticking out of its torso.

No one spoke as they rode out of Devil's Backbone. They reached the exit and traveled through the Pollard's Lumber parking lot and across the highway.

"What happened?" Slade asked as he slowed to a coast.

Kevin pedaled past him. "I saw it again! Just follow me."

"What did you see?" Larry yelled. "Follow you where?"

"DQ," Kevin said.

They tailed him without question. Kevin threw his bike down in front of Dairy Queen and jerked the door open.

The rest followed suit.

The elderly men sat at their normal table playing cards. Bill, Frank, and Jesse, who had talked with them before, all turned as Kevin barreled in.

He breathed heavily.

Bill set his cards down. "What in the Sam Hill's got you so worked up?"

Larry, Slade, and Rut wanted to know as well.

Kevin spurted out several sentences explaining their plans to solve the Claymore murder case and their walk through the house that led upstairs to the little girl's room. "And then I saw it."

"Ya saw what?" Bill asked.

"A ghost," Kevin said. He said it quietly but with a serious tone.

Jesse cupped his ear. "What'd he say?"

"I believe the boy said he saw a ghost out at the Claymore place," Bill said.

"Oh." Jesse nodded, then shook his head. "A what?"

Kevin's friends listened and nodded in support. They'd witnessed the many strange occurrences of the Claymore mansion as Devil's Backbone delivered on the terrifying tales they'd heard in the past.

The old men looked at Kevin as if he were crazy.

Bill scooted his chair back and turned to Kevin. "Now, son, tell me exactly what you saw. And speak up for ole Jesse."

"Well, I've actually seen it twice. Several weeks ago, we were ridin' by, and I saw it in the upstairs window just starin' back. Then one night this light came on. Today, I saw it in the back by a shed holdin' a knife. It wore this beige outfit. Like coveralls. Long gray hair and a beard." Kevin slowed down and took a breath. "And the worst part—it was holdin' a knife."

Bill's stern look slowly morphed into a smile and then a full-blown laugh. Frank, Jesse, and the other men joined him in laughter.

Kevin frowned. "What the heck. What's so funny?"

The other teens looked at one another, confused.

Bill wiped his eyes and coughed as his laughter ended. "Son, you didn't see no ghost. You saw Dickie Claymore."

Kevin's jaw dropped. "Wha . . . how?"

"You saw Dickie Claymore," Bill repeated. "It's his house. He lives there."

Kevin argued, "But you said that after he came back from the war, he lived with the sheriff's wife. I just thought that was it. Maybe he died or somethin'."

"Well, y'all ran out of here to go play ball or something before I finished," Bill said. "The sheriff's wife passed away in the late twenties. Dickie decided it was time he moved on out to his folk's place. Been there the last fifty years. Kind of a recluse. You know what that means?"

Kevin shook his head as the other teens stood around him.

"Means he lives by himself and tends to avoid other people. He just never took to getting married or really getting to know anyone. Like we said before, the murders changed him. He was a victim too. Never saw someone so full of life as young Dickie. But the life just sorta went out of him." Bill dropped his head.

"Any of you kids ever seen that beat-up, old, blue, '55 Ford pickup drivin' into town on occasion?" Frank asked.

Slade's eyes lit up. "Yes, sir! I've seen it by my dad's office. Guy with long white hair and beard . . . ohhh." His voice trailed off in realization that he'd seen Dickie many times before.

"So that's Dickie," Kevin said, acknowledging the fact. Telling the ghost story embarrassed him, but at the same time, he was relieved to be free of the supernatural. He held up a finger. "But, what about the knife? Seemed like he was crazy or somethin'."

"Nah," Frank answered. "He was probably just butcherin' a hog or somethin'. He hunts quite a bit. Wild hogs, deer, quail, stuff like that."

"Hee, hee. Sounds like you kids owe Dickie an apology for running around his house," Jesse said. "Y'all best get out there before he calls the sheriff on you."

Kevin's shoulders slumped.

Rut slowly shook his head.

"Um . . . can you go with us?" Kevin asked.

Bill pulled his chair back toward the table and chuckled. "Nah. You kids made this bed; now ya gotta lie in it. You don't need us nohow. He won't hurt ya none if that's what you're thinking. Some folks think he's crazy. Kinda looks it. But he's harmless."

Frank scoffed. "Well, lucky he didn't shoot at 'em. He don't take too kindly to folks runnin' around his property. That's why nobody hunts down there."

Bill swatted at him. "Nah. Y'all don't listen to Frank. I'm sure Dickie knew y'all meant no harm. He probably doesn't care 'bout a bunch of you kids running around."

Wendy had remained silent. Arms folded. Pondering. "Wait a

minute. Somethin' still ain't right. That house just looks haunted. It's so old. And inside was really weird. It was like we were in a time machine. Like no one's been there for a hundred years or somethin'."

"You just hit the nail on the head, little lady." Jesse rubbed his chin. "I'll betcha not a single soul's been in that house since the murders. Other than Dickie, of course. After the Texas Rangers did their investigation, Sheriff Brown hired me and another feller to cover up the furniture and board up the windows. After we finished, I walked out the front door, locked it, and gave the key to the sheriff. When these other folks came to investigate the murders, amateurs and such, the sheriff wouldn't let them in.

"When I heard Dickie had moved out there, round about 1928 or so, I took a ride out there. He had taken the boards off the windows and cleared out some brush. Busted the sod off to the side for a garden.

"One thing he didn't have to do is clean up the cemetery. A few of us took it upon ourselves to keep that cleaned up. But Dickie does it now."

"Didn't Dickie ever do anythin' about the investigation? Ever try to solve it?" Kevin asked.

"Funny you say that," Bill answered. "Dickie don't really talk to anybody when he's in town. Just keeps to himself. If you say 'howdy' to him, he'll say 'howdy' back, but that's about it. Well, about twenty years ago, there was these fellers walking out of the cafe, and they were talking about the murders. One feller would say that two guys did it with pistols and another feller said it was one guy with a rifle.

"Well, they didn't know Dickie was standing right by them, listening. He interrupted them and said, 'There was three of them. One shotgun. That's it.'

"That's all Dickie said. He turned around and walked off. Tons of rumors about Dickie like he's crazy and such, but he doesn't seem to care none. But I guess he don't like anyone saying anything wrong about his family or what happened to them."

Kevin's heart sank. The chill rippled down his back. His eyes widened. He looked at Wendy and then his other three friends, one by one.

They looked back at him with no alarm or emotion. They apparently failed to grasp what he had.

Kevin realized they possessed the murder weapon. The shotgun they found on the first day of building the fort. The one they all had played with. The one with the Pollard's Raiders emblem they had researched. And now, this vital piece of evidence to the murders rested in a hollowed-out tree.

"Uh . . . I just remembered. We have to go," Kevin said.

The other teens looked at him.

"Why?" Larry asked.

Kevin gave a stern look. "We just do." He nudged toward the door with his head. "Thank y'all for tellin' us those stories."

"Yeah, thanks," Wendy said.

Bill lifted his hand. "Don't mention it. Come back anytime."

Frank, Jesse, and the other men turned to their card game.

CHAPTER 16

"WHAT'S THE BIG hurry?" Larry asked, loudly.

"Shush. Y'all just c'mon. I'll tell you in a minute."

They rode from DQ into town following Kevin. He stopped in the alley between the Ben Franklin 5–10 store and Pollard's Hardware. Kevin dropped his bike and turned on a water spigot for a drink.

The others followed suit, taking turns at the spigot for a drink of warm, almost hot, water.

"So, what's the big mystery? No ghost. It's just Dickie Claymore. This whole time we've been runnin' around scared of nothin'," Slade said.

Kevin wiped his mouth. "It's that last part that Mr. Bill talked about. Dickie said the murders were committed by three guys with one shotgun. Don't y'all get it?" Kevin waved his arms, palms up. "We have the murder weapon. The shotgun that was buried. The murderers obviously buried it there. We found the murder weapon."

"What? Bull crud," Rut said.

Slade rolled his eyes.

"Wait a minute. Why is that so crazy?" Larry asked. "We

already know it's not from the Civil War battle. Why else would a shotgun be buried out there? Think about it. What do murderers do? They always try to get rid of the evidence."

Wendy had stooped for an unladylike drink from the spigot and rose. "Remember what that Jefferson Pollard over at the lumber store said to us? He said that veterans from that Pollard's Raiders would put that emblem on patches for their hats and coats and stuff. And plaques on their walls too. Maybe one of them put it on their shotgun. And they're the murderer, or one of 'em at least." She pointed her finger with authority.

"But we ain't even sure it's the same symbol. I mean it kinda looks like it," Slade said.

"We should go to the state historical marker and gravestone rub it. Then we'll go to the fort and compare it to the shotgun," Kevin said.

"Do what?" Rut asked.

"Gravestone rub it," Larry answered. "You'll probably do that in school next year. It's where you take, like, thin paper and hold it on the gravestone, then rub it with a crayon. It makes a copy of it. We did it in school this year."

"Creepy." Wendy shivered. "Hated that."

Kevin nodded. "Yeah, that way we'll have a picture of it. We can go look around town and see if it's anywhere else. We need to see how many of these Pollard's Raiders things are still around."

Creak.

Larry and Slade looked up over Kevin.

Kevin looked to his left at a shadow as if it were standing next to him. He turned. In his head, whistling music played from a Clint Eastwood western he'd seen.

Most of Mead Creek's storefronts had paved sidewalks, but the area in front of Pollard's Hardware had an elevated wooden deck, a throwback to another century.

Ephraim Pollard towered over the five teens. His fedora tipped slightly to the side, and he squinted one eye. He wore a white, long-sleeved, button-down shirt, black slacks, and brown, scuffed shoes. Not expensive clothes but K-Mart from head to toe. "What in the hell you kids doin' there?"

"Uh . . . just gettin' a drink," Kevin answered.

"I can see that. I mean what are you talkin' about?" he asked with a sharp tongue. "I heard you say somethin' about Pollard's Raiders. 'Bout them doin' somethin'."

Kevin looked at Slade and Larry for help but they gave none. Wendy shrugged.

Rut looked in the opposite direction as if his mind was elsewhere.

Kevin weighed his options. He didn't know how much the old man had heard. He knew he was one of the Pollard family and that he had a reputation for snapping at people, especially kids that rode their bikes down the sidewalk as they had weeks before. Kevin decided to play out the previous lie. "Well, we found this canteen out in the woods by Meyer's Pond and thought it might be from the Civil War. We saw that historical marker out there on the highway. Just learnin' about the Battle of Mead Creek and stuff and whether it was true what that marker said."

"You kids don't know shit from Shinola. And you sure as hell don't know nothin' about Pollard's Raiders."

Most considered Ephraim Pollard the leader of the town even though his younger brother, Marty "Stump" Pollard, served as mayor. Folks would say that Mayor Stump didn't make a move without consulting Ephraim, who held majority ownership of the hardware store and lumber yard near the entrance to Devil's Backbone.

Ephraim was named after his grandfather, E. M. Pollard, famed leader of Pollard's Raiders and one of the first businessmen in Mead Creek.

E. M.'s son, Marshall, and father of Ephraim and Mayor Stump, had earned a trip to Huntsville Prison for manslaughter after an altercation with a local banker. Dickie Claymore's father served as prosecutor. The family carried on due to the fortitude of Ephraim's mother. She ran the store with shrewdness and the family with a firm grip. They'd hoped Marshall would make parole, but he died in prison after a long illness. Ephraim, Stump, and their sister all married and kept their roots in Mead Creek.

Ephraim's one son, J. C. Pollard, pastored the First Baptist Church of Mead Creek. Ephraim sat in the second pew next to his wife every Sunday but never attended Sunday evening or Wednesday evening services. When his wife passed away two years prior, he stopped going altogether.

He took two steps closer to the five teens and pulled a pack of Camel cigarettes from his front shirt pocket. He tapped an unfiltered cigarette on his watch to pack it, lit it with a gold Zippo lighter, and blew smoke. He coughed. Not the way Kevin had the first time he smoked; his was an old man cough. "Let me tell you somethin' about Pollard's Raiders," he said with a snarl.

They'd never seen Ephraim sitting with the other elderly men at Dairy Queen and he certainly didn't have their flair for storytelling.

He pointed at Kevin with his cigarette sticking out through his fingers. "Pollard's Raiders saved this town. Them damn Yankees were comin' here to attack. They'd've come in here, shootin' up the town, stealin' goods, done God-knows-what to the womenfolk, and set every buildin' afire. My granddaddy met 'em head-on and whooped 'em. That's what he done. Saved this town, by gummit.

He was a hero. That was Pollard's Raiders and don't let no one tell ya no different."

Wendy scrunched her face, confused. "Wait a minute."

All four boys widened their eyes and turned to her. How dare she challenge the elderly Pollard?

She continued, "Mrs. Oberlin at the library said they were just retreatin' soldiers from another battle. Battle of Mansfield or somethin' and they were just waterin' their horses. How do you know they were comin' to attack Mead Creek?"

The four boys turned their heads back to Pollard in this verbal tennis match.

Now Pollard widened his eyes. "You shut your smart mouth right now, missy. You don't know nothin' and neither does that snot-nosed librarian. And another thing, that dang historical marker out there still don't have it right. Pollard's Raiders saved this town. That's what it oughta say."

Wendy folded her arms and huffed.

"I told you kids not to hang around here. Now git."

In reality, he had never told them not to hang out in that alley. However, it was their sign to leave. They offered no parting greetings or yes sirs. They simply picked up their bikes and walked them away from the store.

Slade sneered and kept a careful eye on Pollard.

The old codger sneered back.

Kevin looked into the hardware store window. Two older faces stared and followed his path.

They mounted their bikes and began riding toward the center of town.

"How long was he standin' there?" Wendy asked.

"Dunno," Larry said. "Hope he didn't hear us talkin' about the murder and the shotgun."

"Probably not. He probably would've said somethin'," Kevin reasoned.

"Man, I was about to tell that old dude to screw off," Slade said.

"Sure, sure you were," Wendy said. "Then you would've whooped him right there. A hundred-year-old man or however old he is."

All but Slade laughed.

"All right. Let's meet tomorrow like usual. We'll go check out the historical marker and then compare it to the shotgun," Kevin said.

"But tomorrow's the Fourth of July," Rut said. "What about the parade and fireworks?"

"We'll be back in time," Wendy said.

"And we have to go meet Dickie," Kevin said.

The others looked at him.

"You know we got to. We got to apologize. Plus, ain't you curious to meet him?"

"Nope," Slade said. "I'm good. I'd rather go to the Oz and play *Space Invaders*."

"Well, you're goin'. We're all goin'," Larry said.

WILLIAM "WILLIE" TRAYNOR loaded a thirty-pound bag of fertilizer into a middle-aged woman's trunk. He wore jeans, a white, short-sleeved, button-down shirt, and a green vest with Pollard's Hardware emblazoned on the left. He'd worked for the company his entire life. As a teenager, Ephraim's father, Marshall Pollard, hired him to sweep, stock shelves, and load goods in the back of customers' wagons. He'd never advanced much more beyond stock boy. Some thought he might be of simple mind, but most knew he simply lacked any ambition.

Traynor married late in life to a woman ten years his senior, a mother to a three-year-old son from her previous relationship. The family never left Mead Creek. Not even for a day trip to Dallas. She died after only two years of marriage. Some said she died of a broken heart over her son's father. Traynor had adopted the boy, given him his name, and raised him as best he could. Having a little more ambition than his father, Raymond Traynor served as Mead Creek's sheriff.

Willie Traynor seemed content to work at Pollard's six days a week for decades and stayed in a garage apartment two blocks south of town. For a man just over eighty years old, he was healthier and fitter than most his age. He attended church on occasion as well as other town functions, but he preferred a life with no stress and no challenges. He'd stayed close to Ephraim Pollard his entire life, as the two were only four months apart in age. They played in the same woods as kids and attended the town's only school, where Traynor was lowest in the pecking order, and Pollard was at the top.

Once Ephraim began managing the hardware store, he made sure the pecking order continued and oversaw the teen with a harsh demeanor. The subservient Traynor obeyed, and that relationship never changed over the years. He officially retired years ago but asked to stay on part-time to keep his "spirits up" as he said. Locals liked him, and many came to the store for his expert advice on the right plumbing part or the best fertilizer for a St. Augustine lawn.

He stepped up on the sidewalk toward Ephraim Pollard. "What was that about?"

"What was what about?" Pollard barked. He dropped his Camel and rubbed it out with his shoe.

"All them kids you was fussin' at, Ephraim," Traynor said.

Pollard folded his arms and watched the five ride away across the center of town. "They was goin' on and on about Pollard's

Raiders. Askin' questions. They was askin' about things they shouldn't."

"What's wrong with askin' about the Raiders? Heck, they're famous in this town. Why I'd tell them about—"

"That ain't what I mean, Willie. I heard 'em talkin' about playin' out there in the woods. Over by Meyer's Pond. Said they found somethin'. Thought it was from the Civil War or some such. But I could tell they was lyin'. I think they're up to no good. I got a mind to look into it."

"Into what, Ephraim? Just a bunch of kids. You oughta rethink that. They don't mean no harm."

Pollard tapped another Camel on his watch. "We'll just see about that."

CHAPTER 17

THEY POURED WITH sweat after the uphill bike ride to the state historical marker on the highway. Even at 10:30 in the morning, the temperature had already neared ninety degrees.

Wendy supplied the thin paper and crayons with sixty-four color selections.

"Why did you bring so many? We ain't colorin' a picture," Slade said, chuckling.

She shrugged. "Dunno. Just grabbed 'em."

"Slade brought somethin' else." Rut snickered.

"What?" Wendy asked.

"Oh, nothin'," Slade answered.

"C'mon, what?" she insisted.

Slade held up a water jug. "Let's just say the old man won't miss a couple of Coors beers."

"Really," Larry said. "You stole beer to drink at ten in the mornin'?"

"Nah. I added a bunch of ice. Thought we might take a few swigs before the parade tonight."

"Ooh, yeah," Rut said.

"I don't think so," Wendy said. "You ain't drinkin' no beer.

No way."

"Guys! Forget the beer. We've got serious work to do." Kevin had dismounted from his bike and stood next to the marker.

Wendy held up the paper, and Kevin rubbed the crayon across the Pollard's Raiders emblem. The Stars and Bars of the Confederacy emerged, as did the name of the militia group. "Pollard's" arched across the top and "Raiders" curved in the opposite direction under the Stars and Bars. Two muskets crossed one another with the letter C on one side and "6th" on the other. The marker stated that Pollard's Raiders served in the 6th Battalion, Cavalry, State Troops.

"Dang! I didn't think it would work, but it really shows it," Larry said. He held it out and compared it with the emblem on the marker. "It's almost like a Polaroid."

Kevin took the rubbing from him, folded it, and stuck it in the back pocket of his Wrangler cutoffs. "All right, let's go to the fort."

Four of them pointed their bikes down the highway from where they had come.

Slade pointed his toward the supposed shortcut. "Where y'all goin'? This way's quicker."

"Are you kiddin' me?" Wendy asked. "Last time it took us forever, and we had to cross the creek."

"Yeah, but now we know where we're goin'," Slade offered. "Trust me. We'll get there quicker."

Kevin looked at Larry and shrugged. "It probably would be quicker. But, I'll lead this time. I remember the way."

The line of bikes meandered through infrequently traveled trails toward Mead Creek where they stopped, removed their shoes and socks, and waded through the water.

Entering the fort, Slade did his ceremonial kiss of the hand and touch to the lips of Cheryl Tiegs, who hung from an interior wall.

Wendy and Rut took their seats as everyone typically sat in the same spot.

Outside, Larry and Kevin walked toward the hollowed-out tree that stored the shotgun.

"I'll get it," Kevin said.

Larry walked to the fort.

"It's gone!" Kevin yelled. "It's gone! The shotgun's missin'."

Wendy looked at Slade. "All right, what did you do with it?"

Slade held up his hands. "What do you mean? I didn't do anythin' with it."

Larry ran over to the tree and looked for himself. "It's gone."

The other three joined them at the tree.

"All right, who talked?" Kevin asked.

"What d'ya mean?" Rut asked.

"It's obvious somebody told someone else about the shotgun, and they came and got it. So, who told somebody?" Kevin looked each one in the eye.

"I didn't tell no one. I swear," Rut said.

"Not me," Wendy said.

Everyone looked at Slade.

He looked back and shook his head. "I swear. Didn't tell nobody."

Larry gave Kevin a mature cock of the head. "You know I didn't tell anyone."

"All right. So, nobody told anyone. Let's check for clues. Look for footprints," Kevin ordered.

"Seriously?" Slade asked.

"Yes. Seriously," he answered. "Don't you see? We may have found the weapon to an unsolved murder, and now someone else got it. They might know somethin'. Maybe they're coverin' up for the murderer."

"Wait a minute," Rut said. "This was like a hundred years ago. No one would still be tryin' to cover this up."

Kevin held up a finger. "It was sixty-seven years ago, and that's exactly what I'm sayin'. Keep lookin'."

After two minutes of dedicated searching, they found nothing. No footprints. No trampled grass or broken twigs.

"Look, Kevin. We ain't findin' nothin'," Wendy said.

"Well, guess we'll just go see Dickie," Kevin suggested.

"Are we gonna tell him about the shotgun?" she asked.

Kevin shrugged. "Dunno. Maybe. We'll see."

———— • ◉ • ————

NONE OF THEM really wanted to go meet Dickie. At least none of them showed any enthusiasm at meeting this elusive figure they'd spent many conversations pondering over. They'd heard the DQ Bunch speak of him fondly, but even Kevin had called him a ghost. They now realized he wasn't that, but he was a mystery. A recluse. A storied figure like none they'd ever dealt with before. Their toughest adversary so far had been Ephraim Pollard. Maybe Wayne Moretti at the arcade.

Kevin's mind raced as they rolled past the Claymore cemetery. The men at DQ assured them that Dickie was harmless. But Kevin and friends had broken into his home, not once, but twice. Kevin and Wendy had walked around inside. Dickie might want to have them arrested. They could just ride past the mansion and forget anything ever happened. They could simply never return to the fort. No one would ever really know.

The other four stopped, giving Kevin no choice.

As they had done many times before, they lined their bikes along the Devil's Backbone road across from the Claymore mansion. It looked no different than before. That didn't make it any less frightening. Not only would they have to face the real Dickie Claymore, but a triple murder had happened there. Those ghosts might still lurk about. Dickie might be living with ghosts. Two wills raged in Kevin's head. One wanting to flee and one desiring to meet the mysterious man and solve the murder.

"Well, Kevin. Mr. Tough Guy. You dragged us out here. Guess you should be the one to go meet that old Dickie dude," Slade said.

Kevin looked at him in denial.

"No! We're all goin'." Larry threw his leg over his bike and dropped it, roughly. "Let's go," he said, matter-of-factly.

The other four followed Larry's demand and dropped their bikes.

They walked in rank like soldiers with Larry a half-step ahead. No one spoke. The sun, directly overhead, beat down on them. Aside from the occasional fire ant pile or clump of weeds, they walked across dirt that had at one time been Mrs. Claymore's finely manicured front lawn.

They stopped at the bottom step to the porch.

"Let's go," Kevin declared.

He took the first step as the others followed, and all five slowly made their way up the steps.

Wendy grabbed Rut's arm, pulling him to the side before he stepped through a hole in the porch.

The door that had slammed shut on Rut and that Kevin and Wendy had escaped through towered before them. It was no ordinary front door. The massive wooden piece had intricate inlays in each panel and appeared wider and taller than the typical door in these teens' tract home neighborhood. The door knocker stared back at them. A face they couldn't make out. Attached was a round knocker the size of a baseball.

Kevin looked at Wendy and then reached for the knocker.

"You young ones looking for me, I suppose." The voice came from their right. A deep, authoritative voice.

Wendy wanted to scream but covered her mouth.

Rut jumped behind her.

Slade and Kevin looked but said nothing.

Larry cleared his throat. "Yes, sir."

Dickie Claymore wiped his brow with a red rag and stuffed it into the back pocket of his one-piece beige utility suit. The butcher knife that Kevin had seen in his hand before had been replaced by a crescent wrench. His dress was that of a working man; he didn't have a wild man or hobo look. His white hair and beard, although long, were trimmed and combed.

Kevin walked down from the porch, suddenly unafraid of the mysterious figure. At ground level, Dickie didn't seem any taller than a normal man. His eyes didn't pierce Kevin's skull. He didn't grasp the wrench to use as a weapon. He was simply an old man, although the picture of health. The top of his cheeks were slightly sunburned.

Dickie smiled. He wiped his free hand on his pant leg and then extended his hand toward Kevin. "Pleased to meet you. I'm Richard Claymore Jr. But the people around here call me Dickie."

Kevin shook his hand. "I'm . . . uh . . . Kevin."

Dickie nodded and then looked at the other four still on the porch.

Kevin pointed to them, one at a time. "That's Slade, Rut, Larry, and Wendy." Each returned the greeting with a head nod.

"So, what brings you kids out here today?" Dickie asked.

Kevin had noticed that Dickie spoke differently than other people that age. His speech was clear and refined. Proper. Free of a Texas twang.

Dickie crossed his arms behind his back and slightly bent

toward Kevin.

"Well, sir, I—" Kevin looked at his friends and back to Dickie. "—I mean, we all just want to say sorry for goin' in your house."

"Well, what were you looking for if you don't mind me asking?"

"It's kinda stupid, but, we thought your house was, uh, haunted and—"

Dickie roared with laughter. "Haunted. Yes, I've heard that one many times before. I'll bet you thought I was a ghost as well. Didn't you?"

Kevin nodded, sheepishly.

"Well, how do you know I'm not?"

Kevin's eyes widened.

"I'm kidding you." Dickie's laugh subsided. "Phew. It is hot out here. How would you kids like a cold drink?"

They all nodded. The other four had yet to say a word.

"Come on around back then."

They followed Dickie toward the back. Although full of life, he waddled a little as he walked.

Kevin looked back at his friends following him as he followed Dickie.

Slade whispered to Rut, and Rut shrugged.

He pointed toward the massive tree that shaded the back of the house. "There are some folding chairs on the porch. Why don't you take a seat in the shade?"

They did as told.

Dickie emerged from the house holding a tray with six blue Solo plastic cups filled with ice and set them on a bench next to the tree. He turned on the spigot and dragged a green water hose toward them with the water at a trickle. He had put on a tan ball cap with a blue brim and a Ford emblem on the front.

They held out their cups as he filled them one by one. Then he filled one for himself.

"Sorry I don't have lemonade or soda for you kids. I don't receive visitors here and don't really invite anyone. But you five seem harmless enough."

"Thank you," Wendy said.

"Well, you're most welcome, young lady. Do you other three boys speak?"

Rut nodded.

"Yes, sir," Larry and Slade said, simultaneously.

"So, tell me more about why you think this old house is haunted," Dickie said with a smile.

Larry whispered to Kevin, "Tell 'em."

"Well, sir. We heard about what happened here. When you were just a kid."

Dickie's smile waned. He looked off to the side. "I see. And you thought that you might go inside and see a ghost, I suppose?"

"Not exactly." Having moved past that awkwardness, Kevin gained confidence and moved to the edge of his lawn chair. "We . . . or at least I thought there might be a ghost. See, we didn't know you lived here. We didn't think anyone lived here. But we wanted to see inside to investigate . . . you know . . . the murders."

"I understand. You certainly aren't the first ones. Amateur sleuths that is. They've been trying to solve this for sixty-seven years. I quit letting them look around back in the 1920s. I simply thought it not worth the time. It's hard for me, you understand, to relive all that."

"We're sure sorry, sir. We didn't mean to . . . you know," Wendy said.

"Don't you worry about that. I know you didn't mean any harm. Plenty of adults have other motives, though. Trying to make a name for themselves. About ten years ago, a news crew from Houston came out here trying to interview me. I ran them off because they just wanted ratings for their news program."

"What if someone could solve it? Wouldn't you want to know?" Larry asked.

Dickie took a long drink from his water cup. "Let me show you kids something."

CHAPTER 18

L IBRARIAN KIM OBERLIN exited the library with her purse draped over her arm. Although the heat deterred most, she enjoyed walking the four blocks home for lunch after staring at books for hours.

Ephraim Pollard sat on a bench in front of the library and spoke as she reached the bottom step. "Excuse me, missy. I got a word or two for ya."

Pollard had recently turned eighty-two, and like Willie Traynor, he remained in excellent health. A clinical eye attributed this to his daily walks around town. Some suggested his crankiness and desire to control others gave him a purpose in life.

"Well, hello, Uncle Ephraim. Looking for a good book?"

"Nope. Not much of a reader. Take a seat here."

She paused, nodded, and politely sat at the other end of the bench. "So, what's brought you over to the library to see me?"

He grabbed the top of his fedora, removed it, and wiped his brow with his forearm sleeve. A tree shaded the spot, but the temperature still felt like it was in the mid-eighties. "Do I need a reason to come see family?"

"Family?" she scoffed. "We've hardly ever spoken."

"Still. You're my little sister's grandbaby. You're family. And family should look after one another."

"Ohhhkay. You came over here just to tell me that?"

He looked left and right. "I had a bunch of them kids messin' around by the hardware store. Overheard 'em talkin' about diggin' around out in those woods by Meyer's Pond and found somethin'. They said they talked to you about it."

She looked puzzled. "Yes, they said they found a canteen and thought it was from the Civil War. I told them about the historical marker and a little about the skirmish. Why would you care about any of that?"

"A canteen, ya say?"

"Why? Why do you care?" She sat her purse on the bench and crossed her legs.

"I had to straighten them out on what really happened. Weren't no skirmish. It was a battle." He began to raise his voice. "You don't mess with history. What's done is done. That's what you should be tellin' 'em. Not sayin' a skirmish." He frowned, crossed his arms, and looked to the side. "And you should tell 'em to mind their own business about such things."

"Uncle Ephraim, I really don't understand why you're getting so worked up about this. They're a lot more interested in the Claymore murders than anything."

He whipped his head toward her.

"They've been riding their bikes down Devil's Backbone and are curious about the house. Do you find that concerning as well?"

"Yes, I do. Why would they want to know about that?"

She shrugged. "They're kids. It's a scary-looking house. To them anyway. And, an unsolved murder. Why wouldn't they be interested?"

He pointed at her. "Like I said, what's done is done. It's history."

He measured his gravelly voice but then pulled back to a normal tone. "I mean, it's sad what happened to that family. A cryin'-ass shame. But they oughta be careful runnin' around out there."

She shook her head in disagreement. "Seems harmless enough. Kids have been playing in those woods for years. Besides, as a teacher and librarian, I love that they're taking the time to learn some history rather than wasting time and money at Oz's Arcade."

He pointed at her again. "They need to stay away from that Claymore place. That Dickie Claymore ain't right in the head. Ever since he came back from the war, he's been all messed up in the head. A loner. Won't talk to nobody. Just sits out in that old house doin' God-knows-what. Hell, he might be dangerous for all we know."

She crossed her arms. "I'd say that if, and I mean if, anything is wrong with him, it would be from seeing his whole family murdered. Grandma said he was changed from that. He was just a normal boy but afterward seemed near catatonic at times."

He rubbed his chin. "Yeah, yeah. You see, that's it. Some folks think he might be the murderer."

"Really? What was he . . . twelve years old? Why would a twelve-year-old, seemingly happy boy, murder his family? Hmmm?"

Pollard circled his finger around his ear suggesting that Dickie Claymore was crazy.

She stood. "Well, Uncle Ephraim, as delightful as this has been, I really do need to get home and meet my husband for lunch."

"Uh-huh. You married that young preacher, right? Donald?"

She corrected him. "David, and you know very well he's the youth pastor."

He tipped his hat toward her as she turned and walked away.

⸺⸺⸺ •◉• ⸺⸺⸺

KEVIN AND FRIENDS left their chairs and cups behind as Dickie led the way past the garage and toward the road.

"Where we goin'?" Kevin asked.

"The cemetery," Dickie said.

They looked at one another.

Once they'd shaken hands, Kevin felt comfortable with Dickie. The DQ men assured them he wasn't crazy or dangerous. However, following a strange old man to a cemetery opposed his sense of reason and safety.

A black, wrought-iron fence, free of rust, enclosed the small cemetery. There seemed only room for four or five other graves. Unlike the house and grounds around the mansion, the cemetery was free of debris and weeds. The three gravestones leaned to one side or another and showed weathering, but this was a well-kept area. They could easily see over the fence, as it stood only four feet tall.

Dickie removed his ball cap.

Slade, the only other one wearing a hat, caught the hint and removed his as well.

The stones showed the full names of Richard, Clara, and Ruth Claymore, their years of birth, and the same year of death, 1912.

Kevin had seen something similar at the large Mead Creek cemetery south of town. Entire families buried the same year. His father told him they likely all died of the same disease. Sad, yes, but the Claymore deaths carried a much greater weight.

Dickie touched Larry's shoulder. "So, young man, you asked me, if someone could solve their murders, would I want to know? Let me ask you. Do you think they want to know?" Dickie nodded toward the graves.

No one spoke.

A tear rolled down Wendy's cheek.

"Yes!" Kevin announced. "They would want to know."

Dickie nodded. "I agree. It wouldn't bring them back, but it would certainly serve justice to know who did it and why they did it."

Dickie sat on a patch of grass.

The five teens followed suit.

Several trees provided ample shade. A breeze comforted them. Not a cool breeze, but it wasn't a hot one either. Just enough to blow their sweat-drenched hair off their foreheads and keep the flies away.

Although Dickie had longer hair than most men, Kevin noticed the bald spot on his crown.

Dickie cleared his throat. "One time I asked my daddy why he was a lawyer. He said that he wanted to be a voice for those that couldn't speak for themselves. Sometimes a victim or someone wronged doesn't have the means to fight. They don't have the money or don't know how to seek justice. Or they're no longer with us.

"He'd say it was kind of like a bully picking on someone. He was the bystander that stopped the fight and stood up to the bully. I'd always smile when he said that. I was glad that there were people willing to stand up to bullies. I read this book a while back. *Lord of the Flies*. It shows what happens when no one stands up for the weak. That was my daddy. Standing up for the weak. My hero."

No one spoke for several seconds. A moment for reflection.

Dickie broke the silence as he looked at his father's headstone. "We have lots of conversations about this. I've asked my daddy a thousand times who did it. Who gunned him down in front of the house? I ask my mother if she even saw it coming. I don't ask Ruth anything. I don't want to think about that."

Slade looked at Dickie with concern.

Dickie offered a slight grin. "Don't worry. I'm not actually talking to them, and they aren't actually speaking back. It's more of a theoretical conversation. Trying to trigger my memory about what I saw."

Kevin sat with his knees to his chest and his arms around his legs rocking. "We've heard stories from all those guys at Dairy Queen and even read some of the old newspaper reports. The paper said you were in your room readin' when it happened and escaped down the side of the house. You must've been so scared."

"More than you can imagine," Dickie answered. "You know, I haven't talked to anyone about this since I was your age. Like I said before, plenty of reporters have tried to contact me as well. Mrs. Brown, the sheriff's wife, tried to get me to talk about it for years. Even when I came back from the war. She wanted me to talk about the war too. I saw a lot of bad stuff over in Europe, but nothing compared to what happened to my family. Mrs. Brown and her husband were really good to me, but I simply didn't want to be the scared little kid again."

"Oh, yeah, the paper said you hid in the woods 'cuz you were ashamed," Rut said.

Wendy backhanded him on the arm so hard it knocked him over.

"Ow!" he cried.

Dickie chuckled. "It's okay, sweetie. I know he didn't mean any harm." Dickie had been sitting with his legs extended but pulled his knees to his chest to sit as the teens were. He looked at Rut. "I was ashamed. I told you about my daddy fighting for others. I wanted to be like that. But, I ran. I've asked myself many times what if I could have grabbed some sort of weapon? Anything to beat the guys up and save my mother. Or if I could have gotten my sister and hid her with me."

"Guys?" Kevin questioned. "You saw three guys runnin' away,

right? You were at the edge of the woods and saw three guys runnin' toward Devil's Backbone?"

"Not exactly," Dickie answered. He paused and looked directly at his father's gravestone. "As I was saying before, I've never really talked to anyone about this, but I'm going to tell you kids. I'm getting up there in age, and I want someone to know just in case I pass. Not that there's much that can be done now but just to sort of get it off my chest.

"You see, when it happened, I was in shock. They found me out in the woods babbling incoherently. I don't remember everything, but over time little details keep popping in my head. One detail is for sure, I saw three people running away. Three figures that had to be male from their clothing. I mean, most women didn't wear pants in those days. But, I didn't see them from the woods. I saw them from the house. I never left the house. Not for hours."

Wendy had a look of horror on her face. "You were in the house the whole time?"

Rut, Slade, and Larry looked at Dickie in anticipation of his next words.

Kevin leaned forward. "What? You mean you didn't escape out the back?"

Dickie shook his head. "It seems kind of silly now, but after it happened, I didn't trust anyone and didn't tell the exact story. I just said what I thought they wanted to hear. So, yes, I was hiding in the house the whole time. It's probably better if I show you."

CHAPTER 19

D AVID OBERLIN SPREAD Miracle Whip on a slice of Mrs. Baird's white bread. He liked it thick with a slice of Oscar Mayer bologna and Kraft American cheese. His wife, Kim, preferred a bowl of Campbell's chicken noodle soup, and he lit the gas stove to warm her lunch. Both creatures of habit, they met at home for lunch nearly every day. Just as she only had to walk a few blocks from work to home, he only had to walk three blocks from the church.

She uncharacteristically strolled in ten minutes late for their lunch break. "Sorry I'm late. I just had the strangest conversation with Uncle Ephraim."

"Uncle Ephraim? Was he on one of his long walks, and you bumped into him?"

She stirred her soup in the pan and then sipped from the spoon to check the temperature. "Nope. He was sitting on that bench in front of the library. He came out that way to see me."

They sat at their kitchen table, which shared a room with their couch and television. She recounted the entire conversation with Pollard.

"Okay, that's just weird," David said. "I think he's getting senile."

She looked to the side in thought. "Maybe. That, or he just doesn't have anyone else to be mad at this week. He says he was worried about kids playing out in the woods by the Claymore mansion. Worried about Dickie Claymore."

"Why'd he ask you about that?"

"They told him they had come by the library and asked questions about the Claymore place."

"Huh?" David pushed his plate back. "You know how Ephraim never comes to Sunday service since his wife died?"

She nodded.

"He does come by the church dang near every week to see Pastor J. C."

J. C. Pollard served as the pastor of First Baptist Church and was the only son of Ephraim. In his late-fifties and portly, he delivered a slightly less than fire-and-brimstone sermon each Sunday morning. He preferred the same blue suit and pressed white shirt. He required David Oberlin to don similar dress but allowed him to wear his hair long and dress in jeans during the week. He granted him that accommodation, as David had convinced him he needed to dress somewhat like the youth he ministered to. "Pastors in suits don't minister well in Oz's Arcade," he'd say.

Kim stood and cleared the table. "You mean Uncle Ephraim comes by each week to, like, have coffee with Pastor J. C.?"

"Not exactly. Ephraim barrels in with not so much as a 'how do ya do,' heads right on into J. C.'s office, and shuts the door. J. C. is not typically in the best of moods after their little get-togethers."

"What are they talking about?" Kim asked.

David shrugged. "Any good pastor's office has thick walls. You know, for counseling." David used his fingers to place air quotes around the word counseling.

"How long do they talk?"

"Different every time. Sometimes a few minutes, sometimes an hour. He came by yesterday afternoon. First time in a few weeks. I couldn't hear what they were saying, but it was elevated. Ephraim stormed out. Looked pretty angry."

"Did you ask J. C. about it?"

David stood and stretched. "You kidding? You know how he is. He never wants to talk about stuff like that."

Kim objected, "You're a pastor too. And he has problems just like anybody else. You should talk to him."

David laughed. "You really are a Pollard. Wanting to know everyone else's business."

She smirked. "My grandmother was a Pollard. I'm twice removed from that whole thing." She made a circular motion with her open hand.

"Your dad and J. C. are cousins. Maybe he'd talk to him."

Kim picked up her purse, and David followed her toward the door. "My father hardly talks to anyone, much less to anyone about their feelings. No, you're Pastor David and all that implies. You need to have a little counseling session with J. C. Pollard the church member."

"Uh, yes, ma'am. I'll get right on that. And I'll be sure to report to you the strange goings-on of one Ephraim Pollard." He smiled.

She returned the smile, gave him a kiss, and walked away in the opposite direction.

————— • ◉ • —————

DICKIE STOOD, BRUSHED off his backside, and headed for the mansion, a short walk from the cemetery.

The five teens looked at one another, confused, but then followed suit.

As they walked, Dickie wiped his face with his red rag and returned it to his back pocket.

Kevin had to slow down a few times to avoid passing Dickie, who measured his steps. He didn't seem like someone in a hurry for anything.

Dickie grabbed the front door knob but paused. "Since a couple of you have already been inside, you saw how it looks. All old and dusty. Truth be told, I only use a couple of rooms in the house. Still, though, I'd rather you not touch anything. I like it the way it is. Understood?"

All but Rut nodded.

Wendy cocked her head and widened her eyes toward Rut. "Understand?"

Rut acted startled. "Understand!" He made a face to mock her.

The enormous door knocker looked as uninviting as it had before.

Dickie turned the knob and let them in. As the door swung fully open, daylight filled the foyer.

Kevin and Wendy had experienced this portion of the house.

Slade, Larry, and Rut had never made it past the threshold in their attempt. All three looked left, right, and up.

Above them, a chandelier five feet in diameter hung with several layers of glass pieces.

All of them stared at the ornate fixture.

Dickie looked up as well and then flipped a switch, turning on the chandelier, bringing life to the home.

"Wow," Wendy mouthed.

"My mother had that brought all the way from Italy. Venice, I think. I don't believe I've turned that on in years. I like to live simply." He shut the front door.

Slam!

Rut jumped.

Dickie grasped a handle and slid a large door that disappeared into the wall.

Slade cocked his head.

"Bet you've never seen a door like that?" Dickie said.

Slade shook his head.

"It's a pocket door. Pretty neat, I guess. But wait until you see another door I'm about to show you."

They followed Dickie into his father's office.

Kevin's defense mechanisms signaled him that a mysterious old man in a mysterious old house showing them a mysterious door might mean trouble. However, Dickie gave him a peaceful feeling. The gentle old man offered a vibe of warmth and sincerity. Where Dickie led, Kevin and the others followed.

Similar-looking legal books filled the shelves in Richard Claymore Sr.'s office. A large painting of a fox hunt hung on a rare portion of the walls that didn't contain a filled bookshelf. It seemed the only point of leisure in an office that was geared toward legal work.

Dickie grabbed a book off the shelf. "These are the books I liked. Not all of these are legal books. This one here's a good one. *The Adventures of Huckleberry Finn* by Mark Twain. Any of you ever read it?"

Rut looked surprised. "I read that one. I love that and *Tom Sawyer*."

"Figures," Wendy said. "Ain't they both troublemakers?"

Rut fake-smiled and shook his head at her.

Dickie snickered at their back and forth. "I do like to read. Always have. My mother made us read two hours a day."

"Two hours a day?" Slade questioned.

"Yep. Seems like a lot, but, of course, we didn't have TV back in those days or some arcade. We read a lot and imagined a lot. Kind of made up our own TV programs. I never understood how you kids watch that box so much. I still don't have one and never will."

"So, you've read all these books?" Wendy asked.

"Not the legal ones, but all the others, yes." Dickie pointed to multiple shelves. "There are novels and history and science. Books on art and poetry. And, I still read new books. I was actually in the library a few weeks ago. I saw you kids in there talking to that young lady."

"Mrs. Oberlin," Wendy offered.

"Yes, I suppose that's correct."

Dickie picked up another book and rubbed his hand over the cover, wiping away the dust. "This is the book I was reading that day."

Kevin looked over his shoulder and silently read the title: *Oliver Twist*.

"It's the story of a poor orphan making his way in London." Dickie's mood shifted from one of nostalgia to one of gloominess. "My father was sitting in his chair." Dickie patted the back of a large leather chair tucked up to the desk. "We had just come home from church. My mother had walked in and said something about he had better not be working on the Sabbath.

"He said, 'No, no, Clara. Just making sure I have things in order for court tomorrow. We'll be in for lunch shortly.'

"I looked up and saw her wink at him before she turned and walked out. They were so much in love. I'd catch them winking at each other all the time.

"I heard her yell upstairs, 'Ruthie. Lunch in five minutes.'

"Ruth yelled back, 'Yes, ma'am.'

"I returned to my book. I was sitting in that chair." Dickie pointed to a red velvet chair off to the side of the desk.

The five teens listened intently.

Dickie walked over and sat in the chair still holding the book. "I heard someone yelling my father's name. It didn't seem threatening or anything. Just yelling for my father to come outside. It wasn't all that unusual. I thought it was one of the workers that came out on occasion. Coming on Sunday wasn't normal, though. My mother asked who it was, and my father said something like not to worry, that he'd go see. I buried my head in this book and kept reading.

"Next thing I know, I hear them arguing. I couldn't tell what it was about, but it was definitely getting heated.

"Boom!" Dickie blurted out the sound effect, startling the teens.

Wendy clutched her chest.

Kevin, sitting in one of the other chairs, gripped the armrests.

"I knew it was a gunshot. I ran to the window and saw my father lying on the ground, his chest all red. I saw a blurred figure on the porch but couldn't really tell who or what it was. It all happened so fast. I heard my mother's footsteps but I just decided to hide."

"Where did you hide?" Larry asked.

Dickie pointed at a bookshelf behind the desk. "Right there."

CHAPTER 20

THE FIRST BAPTIST Church of Mead Creek saw 180 in attendance on a given Sunday, making it the largest church in Mead Creek. They held services on Sunday and Wednesday evenings to a much smaller audience. As was typical for most East Texas towns, First Baptist Church had competition from several other churches. In addition to the Baptist offering, one could attend services of the Methodist, Pentecostal, Catholic, Episcopalian, or Lutheran persuasion. The Baptist church started in 1884 with the Pollards serving as one of the founding families. The original building still stood and was used for Sunday school classrooms, but three other expansions had added to the house of worship.

J. C. Pollard was only its fourth pastor and had held the position for twenty-six years. His wife led the choir, one daughter organized children's classes, and another daughter prepared communion cups and wafers. His only son was one semester away from finishing his seminary training and was expected to take over for J. C. after a few years of grooming. The J. C. Pollard family epitomized church service, and many in Mead Creek considered Pastor J. C. the town's spiritual leader.

Knock, knock, knock!

Pastor J. C. looked up over his reading glasses to find his youth pastor, David Oberlin, standing in the doorway. "What can I do ya for, David?" He lowered his head and flipped a page in his large, black, leather-bound Bible in preparation for his Sunday sermon.

Oberlin stepped in and sat on the edge of the loveseat adjacent to the pastor's desk. He rubbed his hands together. "Anything you wanna talk about?"

Pastor J. C. offered a disinterested, "Uh-huh."

David stared at him.

Pastor J. C. looked up, removed his glasses, and leaned back. "Sorry, son. What were you saying?"

"I was just asking how you are. You doing okay?"

The elder pastor smiled. "Well, I s'pose I'm doing just fine. Why ya ask?"

David leaned back in the seat. "I noticed your father coming by every week. Seems like a lot of heated discussions. I don't listen in. I respect the privacy of your office. But just thought I'd ask if it's anything you want to discuss."

Pastor J. C.'s smile waned. "I see." He shrugged. "Well, it's nothing. You stick to ministering to the kids, and I'll handle the adults, okay?"

As David had told Kim, he knew the senior pastor wouldn't be open to a junior pastor's counseling. Still, he didn't expect the condescension. "Look, J. C., we all have problems. How many times have you told me 'sometimes people just need us to listen'? That's all I'm saying. I'm here to listen. Not trying to pry."

"Well, it's nothing we need to talk about. My father is a bitter old man. Not much any of us can do about that." He put his glasses on and returned to his Bible. "You might oughta see why all these youths are running around out in the woods. Seems like they might be getting into some mischief."

David stood and headed for the doorway. "Sure, I'll get right on that," he said in a whisper.

Pastor J. C. offered no reply.

⸻ •◉• ⸻

DICKIE'S POINTING AT the bookshelf directly behind the desk and suggesting it as a place to hide dumbfounded the teens.

"I don't get it," Rut said.

"Let me show you." Dickie pulled three books out from the middle and reached in. The entire bookshelf rotated out forty-five degrees, revealing an opening in the wall. He picked up a flashlight that sat on the floor and slid the switch on. "Come take a look."

The space was little more than the size of a closet with a ceiling twice the height of a normal closet. An attached, wooden ladder ran up the wall. One at a time, they moved sideways through the tight opening.

As they took turns, Dickie explained the unusual feature of the home. "My mother always hated this. Didn't think it was needed. Daddy convinced her that we should have another way downstairs in case of fire. But I knew better. He just liked the idea of having a secret passageway. He also thought we could keep valuables in here."

"Where does it lead?" Kevin asked.

"There's a trap door at the top. It opens in the back of the master bedroom closet. They always made sure nothing heavy was stacked there so you could get in and out."

"Did you use it much?" Rut asked.

Dickie smirked. "Well, enough I guess. Believe me, I wanted to show my friends, but I wasn't allowed to talk about it. Back then, we didn't have flashlights. We had a lantern. I'd get in there and climb up and down. Play like I was a spy or something."

Wendy was the last to look. She stepped out and handed the flashlight to Dickie.

"Just leave it in there. Never know when you might need it," he said.

Kevin looked at Larry and mouthed, "Wow!"

"Anyway, that's where I was. I got in, pulled the bookshelf closed, and just sat there for a minute. Then I heard the front door burst open. I heard my mother scream and then lots of footsteps. I was worried they might find me, so I went up the ladder. I got halfway up and heard another gunshot. I stopped. Just sort of frozen for a minute.

"I heard some of them yelling at each other, but inside these walls, it sounded muffled. Then, I heard them going upstairs. I remembered my sister was probably still in her room. I decided I needed to go get her so she could hide with me. I opened the trap door." Dickie covered his mouth. "Then I heard another shot. Then more footsteps. Then silence. It's almost like I knew. No one was screaming. I waited, maybe two or three minutes."

Dickie left the office and walked back into the foyer.

None of them followed.

He motioned for them. "Guess I better show you the rest of it."

They walked toward the back of the house and stopped near the kitchen.

Dickie knelt down and lightly rubbed the wood floor. "This is where Mother lay." He remained kneeling and rested his hands on his thighs, pausing for a moment of reverence.

They didn't ask questions about his mother. They'd read in the microfilm of the newspaper how she'd been found. A truly gruesome scene.

He pushed up on his knees to stand. "Let's go upstairs."

Wendy remained behind for a few seconds, covering her mouth

and staring at the floor.

Partway up the stairs, Dickie paused at the portrait Kevin and Wendy had pondered. He touched his mother's hair. "She was such a beautiful woman. So refined. Elegant. Caring. I loved her so much."

Kevin's lip quivered.

Slade folded his arms.

They had nothing to say. Nothing could be said.

As they reached the top of the stairs, Dickie turned to the left toward four closed doors. Four to the right were closed as well.

Dickie reached for the black, oval knob of one of the doors and looked back. "This is Ruth's room." He stepped in and let the door open the rest of the way with a creak.

As the teens filed in one by one, Dickie sat on Ruth's bed. He reached for a doll that lay on the pillow and stroked the doll's hair. He pointed behind his back with his thumb. "That's where Ruth was found. She was wearing a pink dress. Her favorite. Mother didn't want her wearing the same dress every Sunday, but she told Mother that all the other girls had to wear the same dress each Sunday because they only owned one. That was Ruth. She just wanted to make friends with the other girls."

Rut shoved his hands in his pockets and stood by the door, seemingly eager to leave.

Kevin dropped to one knee where Dickie had pointed and touched the wood. He nodded, slightly. He didn't do this as Dickie had done, out of reverence. Rather, Kevin acknowledged it as the same spot he had assumed it to be on his last visit to the home.

Dickie never turned, perhaps unwilling to look at the site where his little sister had been ruthlessly murdered. The doll remained in his lap, and he continued to stroke her hair.

Slade and Larry milled about the room as the scene became

more awkward.

Dickie stared out one of the two windows on each side of the headboard. Both sets of drapes had been pulled back.

Wendy sat next to Dickie and rubbed his back. It was as if he was thirteen again.

He looked at her as a tear formed in the corner of his eye. "Thank you, little lady."

Kevin looked out the other window where he had seen Dickie by the outbuilding holding a knife. What he thought was a ghost. The thing that terrified him. The entity that stared back at him from the house. The phantom figure now sat four feet away. Heartbroken. Fully human and comforted by a sweet, fourteen-year-old girl.

After an agonizing forty seconds, Dickie cleared his throat and returned the doll to the pillow. He sniffed and rubbed his finger under his nose. "Let me show you the next thing that happened."

He led them across the hall to the master bedroom. He opened the closet and then the trap door. "After that last gunshot, I heard something like, 'We gotta get!' I heard them shuffling down the stairs. At this point, I didn't know if there were only two of them or several. I was so scared. It was hot in there. Sweat was pouring down me. But I couldn't move. I finally realized I better go see if I could help my family. Even though I heard the gunshots and my mother scream, I still didn't know what all had happened."

Dickie moved toward the window. "I climbed out and ran over here. That's when I saw the three figures running around the corner. To this day, I rack my brain trying to think of who they were. There were definitely three. All male from what I could see. But I only saw them a split second as they ran around that clump of trees." Dickie pointed toward the road. "It's a lot thicker than it was then, but still kind of looks the same."

Dickie put his hand on Kevin's shoulder. "I know you kids

call that road Devil's Backbone, but I prefer its original name: Claymore Lane."

Kevin half-nodded.

Dickie stared out the window and said nothing.

Kevin gently spoke. "What did you do next?"

He looked at Kevin with an empty expression. "That's when it hit me. The silence. I realized there was no noise. No screaming. No talking. No commotion at all. Just quiet. That silence scared me more than when I was in the secret passageway. Because I knew what that silence meant. It meant that my family was hurt. Really hurt. Bad.

"I screamed for Ruth. I ran to her room and found her lying there. Clutching her doll. Her pink dress all messed up. I can't even say . . . I just . . . I just knew she was gone. Her eyes were open. Almost staring back at me just like the lifeless doll. I backed out of her room. Slowly. I whispered, 'Mother.'

"I ran down the stairs and toward the back of the house. Mother lay face down. Motionless. I thought to myself, Daddy might have made it. He was so strong. He was the one that always defended others. Surely, he could help me now. I ran to the front door and shouted, 'Daddy!'

"But he wasn't moving either. I shook my head in disbelief." Dickie shook his head, mimicking his thirteen-year-old self.

The five teens stood around Dickie in the master bedroom, captivated by his story. What began as a knock on the man's door to apologize for trespassing had turned into the most incredible story they'd ever heard.

"You were so lucky," Rut said.

Wendy began to correct him for blurting out what they all were likely thinking.

Dickie nodded. "You know, I've asked myself that a million

times. Was I lucky to survive, or would I have been better off going with my family? I suppose there's a higher power in control of these things."

Dickie reached for the lace on the edge of the bedspread and ran it through his fingers. "I sure am thirsty. Let's go back outside and have a sit. Get a drink."

They followed Dickie to their seats behind the mansion with fresh cups of water.

"So, after you saw your father outside, what did you do next?" Kevin asked.

"I ran back in the secret passageway. Right behind the bookshelf. I just sat there. For hours. I don't know exactly how long. Then it occurred to me that the killer might know me and come back. I came out, ran right past my mother, and out the back door. I ran faster than I'd ever run before. I didn't even know where I was going. I just ran out into the woods.

"This is where the lie came in. I told the sheriff that I escaped before my sister was killed. But it was later that I ran into the woods. Hours later.

"I finally stopped. Exhausted. I don't even know where I was, but it was near the creek. I stuck my head in and lapped up some water. I couldn't really see because the sun was going down. I leaned against a tree and fell asleep. Things are a bit hazy after that. They say I was out in the woods for days. Some father and son that were fishing found me and took me home. Their family lived along the creek. They gave me a bar of soap and told me to bathe in the creek. Said I looked and smelled like an animal."

"For days," Wendy said. "We read about that. You were in the woods for like three days. I bet you were starvin'."

"Probably so," Dickie said. "After that, tons of questions from this grown-up or that grown-up. It all seems like a blur. Then, I was just sort of living with Sheriff and Mrs. Brown. That's what I called them."

Slade chomped on ice and spit it out into his cup. "Did they ever accuse you of . . . you know?"

The other teens looked at Slade, knowing it was a difficult question but one that had to be asked. They turned to Dickie for an answer.

Dickie rubbed his beard. "Still do. I hear whispers when I'm in town. People saying, 'That's the guy that did it,' and things like that. It's hurtful that people would think such a thing.

"Of course, Sheriff Brown never thought that. No. He went to his grave wishing he would have solved it. He never promised me he would. But he swore he'd do everything he could.

"Mrs. Brown was pretty serious about him not working on the Sabbath, but knew he sometimes had police business. He'd be gone for hours on a Sunday, but it's not like there was a bunch of crime. I found out years later from her that he would come out here and look and ponder. Searching for clues."

Kevin opened his mouth to ask another question. "Do—"

"You kids ever seen Suicide Hill?" Dickie asked.

CHAPTER 21

EAST TEXAS HAS its share of endless, flat plains, as well as hills and swamps. Travelers coming from the west will notice the trees getting taller and thicker. The woods near Mead Creek, Texas, fell somewhere in between. Hunters and hikers found some of them impassable and infuriating due to thorny vines, yet mothers sent their kids searching for buckets of blackberries to make delicious pies.

Few dangers lurked in those woods. A wild hog might knock someone down and rip legs open with tusks. Copperhead and cottonmouth snakes could strike after someone overturned a rotten log or stepped into the water. Mead Creek's citizens might occasionally talk of a cougar in the area, and some of the men would attempt to hunt it down or run it off. For the most part, the woods posed no great dangers for humans.

The teens had followed the elderly man to a cemetery. They followed him throughout the house for what was, essentially, a murder tour. Now they followed him through a section of the woods they'd never seen to a location known as Suicide Hill. And they were fine with it. He didn't seem to take any trail but made deliberate steps.

"Ouch!" Wendy cried, as yet another vine's thorns scraped her bare shins.

Slade attempted the *The Three Stooges* routine of pulling a branch and letting it snap back at one of the other boys.

Larry ducked at one of Slade's attempts and the branch passed inches from his face. "Dirtbag!" he shot back at Slade.

They headed in a direction well behind the cemetery, on the opposite side of Meyer's Pond. None of them had ever seen this, and it took them further in the woods than they'd ever gone before.

Somewhat winded, they had trouble keeping up with the old man, who seemed to make the trek with ease. Unknown to them, he'd taken them several hundred yards up a gradual hill. Most of the woods they ventured were flat.

He led them through a clearing as the terrain turned from greenery rocky. Dickie placed his hand on his thigh to step up on naturally formed steps to the top of a massive boulder.

The five followed him and stood with mouths agape.

"Whoa! You can see for miles," Rut said.

"That's right," Dickie said. "We're about a hundred feet higher than down at my place. Most folks have never been here. You can't really see it from the highway because it bends away from it and it's hidden behind the trees. Look this way." Dickie turned them around and pointed. "That little gray piece sticking up out of the trees is my house."

"Oh, yeah," Larry said. "And there's the Mead Creek water tower."

"So this is Suicide Hill?" Kevin asked.

"Nope," Dickie answered. He walked to the other end of the boulder and leaned over.

They followed him, cautiously.

"That's Suicide Hill," Dickie said. "Careful. It kind of sneaks up on you."

They each inched toward the edge.

Slade dropped a rock down the hill and watched it skip and crash to the bottom. "Why do they call it Suicide Hill?"

"Well, some folks would come out here and dare one another to ride their horses down the hill. Most would answer with, 'That's suicide!'"

"Not real nice for the horse either," Wendy said.

"I bet I could ride my bike down that," Slade announced.

"Sure you could," Rut said. "Been nice knowin' ya."

"It doesn't look so hard." Slade moved down the hill a few feet and motioned with his hand. "You just stick to the side and take it slow. Keep on your brakes. You can do it."

"You've got a good eye, son," Dickie said. "That's how I did it on a horse once. Of course, the horse did most of the work."

Slade folded his arms and nodded with a satisfied look.

Dickie knelt, picked up a rock, and tossed it. "You know, you kids remind me of my friends. We spent so much time in these woods. Doing stuff just like this. Exploring. I probably know these woods better than anybody.

"We used to play Civil War. We'd always argue over what side to be on. Everyone wanted to be a Rebel. No one wanted to be a Yankee. But, somebody had to be the enemy. It was a lot of fun.

"Of course, when I went off to war and fought in France, I didn't think it was fun anymore."

Wendy sat down in the middle of the boulder. "Phew."

Evening loomed, but the humidity took its toll.

"Did you have to kill anyone?" Larry asked.

They'd moved past worrying about inappropriate questions.

Dickie placed his arms on his hips and looked down. "Well, son. It was war. Wasn't playing around in the woods."

"Actually, those men at Dairy Queen have told us a lot of stuff," Kevin said. "They told us about you in the war. Said you won medals."

Dickie smirked. "How many Germans did they say I killed? Five? Ten? Twenty?"

"I think it was about nine," Larry answered.

"Well, truth be told, it's not something I'm proud of. I don't boast. I'm not ashamed of it either. I did my part. Those Germans were doing their level best to kill me and my friends. They had us in a tough spot."

"Oh, yeah. They said it was just like bein' in the woods here. You knew it like the back of your hand," Rut said.

Dickie nodded. "You could say that. I had the advantage of knowing the terrain. They had taken over our old trenches so I knew those as well." Dickie knelt down and mimicked moving stealthily. "It was all over in no time."

"Wow! That's so cool!" Larry said.

"Let me tell you the moral of the story. Don't put too much stock in what those boys at Dairy Queen say. They're good fellows, but they tend to embellish. It's sort of their job. Take it all with a grain of salt. I'm betting they told you all kinds of stories about me."

"They did," Kevin said. "But, they were all good stories. They really like you. And your family." Kevin shifted to a somber tone.

"Well, I appreciate that. It was probably that ole Jesse and Frank. Frank was a real good friend. My best friend when I was your age." Dickie picked up another rock and threw it down Suicide Hill.

The four boys took seats on the boulder or on other large rocks.

"I suppose I owe you kids a little confession. I've been watching you go back and forth all summer. For years, teenagers have been coming down that old road. Joyriding or just taking a bike ride to go fish crawdad in the creek. Smoking those funny little cigarettes. Necking or whatever you kids call it." He raised an eyebrow at them. "I occasionally run them off if they try to mess with my house. But like I said before, I know you kids didn't mean any harm.

"I was curious what you were doing down by the creek, and then I saw your little house you built."

"Fort," Kevin corrected him.

"Yes, of course. A fort. After that big storm, I thought it was going to fall over or collapse on you, so I added some boards and made it sturdier. I'll bet you didn't even notice, did you?"

Kevin and Slade shook their heads.

"And you, young lady. What's your name again?" Dickie asked.

"Wendy," she answered.

"I was hunting pigs and saw you walking around away from the creek. Again, I wasn't following you kids, just happened upon you. I saw you needed some privacy so I turned around. But then I heard the pig snort. I was worried he'd run you down so I shot him with my crossbow."

"That was you?" Kevin asked.

"It was. You need to be careful when you're out in the woods and have to squat."

He winked at Wendy.

She blushed.

"I put the pig in a cart and carried it back to butcher him. That day you looked down from inside my house, I was worried what you thought of me holding that big knife. I was just butchering another pig I'd killed. I keep some of the meat and donate the rest to some poorer folks a few miles from here."

"Why do you use a crossbow? Why not a rifle?" Larry asked.

Dickie rubbed his chin. "Well, I guess you could say that I've had enough of guns. I like the silence of the crossbow. More challenging. Nobody likes pigs. They're a nuisance, and folks just want them dead. But I consider them God's creatures. The arrow is more personal. I feel something when I kill one. A little of their pain. Kind of like the war. Not proud. Not ashamed. Just necessary, if that makes sense?"

"Wait a minute," Rut said. "One time we came up and the front door closed all by itself. How did that happen?"

Dickie flashed a devilish look. "Well, an old man has to have a little fun. That was me. After you three ran off, I had a good laugh."

Kevin and Wendy laughed.

Rut, Slade, and Larry didn't.

Dickie rocked himself over and onto a knee to stand up. "It's getting late. We'd better head back."

"Oh my gosh! The parade! We forgot," Rut announced.

"If you call a bunch of old cars and tractors a parade," Slade said.

"You comin', Dickie?"

"Oh, I don't usually go to town for stuff like that. Don't like crowds and the noise from all those fireworks." Dickie stepped off the boulder to lead them back.

* * *

EXITING THE WOODS, they headed toward their bikes as Dickie walked toward his house.

"Can I ask you somethin', Dickie?" Kevin said.

"Sure," he replied.

"Why do you live here? In this big, giant house all alone?"

"That's a good question," Dickie said. "I know the rumors. That I live here and keep it like it was in 1912. That I'm trying to freeze time. That I think my family is still alive and living here. Or that I'm stone-cold crazy. None of that is true. I live here for one reason and one reason only. Because if I don't, the killers win. Simple as that."

CHAPTER 22

"**S**WEETIE!" SLADE'S MOTHER called out as they rode their bikes toward the square.

"Mom. Don't call me that." Slade rolled his eyes.

His parents had arrived early and set up their lawn chairs for prime parade viewing and also for the fireworks that would be set off in the field just south of town.

"Hey, Mr. and Mrs. Littlejohn," Kevin said to Slade's parents.

"Hello, Kevin," Slade's mother said. "Are your parents coming?"

He shrugged. "S'pose to."

Slade's mom touched the back of her hand to her son's cheek. "You're getting too much sun. Maybe you should stay inside tomorrow."

Slade rolled his eyes.

Dozens of others had also placed their chairs on the sidewalk of all four corners surrounding the veterans monument that sat in the center of the town square. Officials set up a barricade at each end of downtown. The parade route would begin at the east end of town and end at the monument, where each parade participant would move to the side for the ceremony.

The program rarely varied from year to year. The parade began thirty minutes before dusk. A band of the only four men in town with the requisite talent played patriotic tunes on a flatbed parked near the monument. The speakers would share their patriotic thoughts followed by mediocre fireworks.

Not a person in town was wowed by the festivities. It was all predictable. And they'd have it no other way.

Kevin spotted his parents parking down the street. "Be right back," he said to his friends.

He ran up to find his father opening the car door of his 1976 Ford LTD.

Smoke billowed out as his dad extinguished a cigarette in the overflowing car-door ashtray. "Howdy, son. What've you been up to all day?"

Kevin shrugged. "Hangin' out. You know."

"Where are your glasses, Kevin?" His mom exited the car.

Kevin had successfully hidden from his friends that he owned a pair of glasses. He often hid them in the bushes in front of his house.

"Uh . . . left 'em at home," he answered.

"Sure, you did," his sister, Becky, said. She stood on the sidewalk with crossed arms and winked at him.

She never missed an opportunity to badger her little brother. They never really fought, but he gave her as much as she gave him. Since she was four years older, their paths rarely crossed in Mead Creek social circles. Her blond locks and status as a cheerleader gave her the popularity that Kevin hoped to have one day.

"The Littlejohns are down there." Kevin pointed toward the square.

"Okay, honey. Help us with these chairs," his mom said.

"Ugh! Is that creepy Slade over there?" Becky asked.

"Yep!" Kevin gladly replied.

"I'm gonna meet my friends." She headed for the other side of the street.

"Suit yourself, honey pie," her father said.

Kevin's parents set up chairs by the Littlejohns and exchanged pleasantries.

Kevin, Slade, Larry, Rut, and Wendy took seats on the curb nearby.

Slade flipped the cap on the jug and swigged. The mix of stolen beer and melted ice made for a warm concoction. He showed a bitter-lemon look.

Rut elbowed Slade. "Dude, your parents are right there," he whispered.

"They just think it's water. Besides, it's nasty now. I don't even want it anymore."

"How do you even know what good beer tastes like?" Rut asked.

Slade smiled.

"Whenever I get my dad a beer, I sneak a sip."

The sun began to disappear behind the west end of town.

The band struck up a chord and played "You're a Grand Old Flag." The drummer banged away as another band member strummed on the guitar propped at the end of his protruding belly.

The first of many convertibles rolled by at ten miles per hour with the occasional tractor or horse mixed in. The volunteer fire department members drove their truck and threw Jolly Rancher candies out for kids to catch.

Several men in partial uniform walked with heads held high, proud of their veteran status. The ninety-nine-year-old Spanish–American War veteran Jacob Carver enjoyed the use of a wheelchair pushed by his son. Some veterans were elderly, and some were middle-aged, except one Vietnam vet who had yet to reach thirty years old. He walked with a limp but had no smile.

The crowd offered polite applause and a few whistled.

Mr. Poteet, manager of the Piggly Wiggly, dressed as a clown and towered over everyone from stilts.

"Mommy, a clown!" one little girl yelled.

Poteet could have walked with the veterans and displayed a chestful of medals for his actions with the 82nd Airborne during the Battle of the Bulge, but he preferred putting smiles on the children's faces.

A tractor appeared to cough, sputter, and stop as the driver, clad in overalls, hopped off and banged the engine with a hammer. Black smoke puffed out. The hillbilly technology somehow did the trick, as his tractor came back to life and resumed the parade route.

"This is so lame," Wendy said. "It's the same thing every year. Same cars. Same tractors. Same songs."

"Yeah, but the fireworks are cool," Rut said.

"I'm so bored with this town. Maybe I should move to Dallas with Dad." She picked up a discarded can and bent the tab back and forth until the ring pull separated from tear strip. She held the ring tab, elbow up, and tried to flick it, but it veered sideway to the ground.

"No way Mom's lettin' ya," Rut announced.

"I'm so bored. So bored with the seventies. I can't wait for the eighties. It'll be so cool. We'll be grown-ups. Can do whatever we want." She worked on another drink tab.

A yellow Cadillac convertible brought up the rear of the parade as Carlisle Laborteaux waved with his right and held a cigar with his left. Mead Creek's most famous son always returned for the Fourth of July parade and typically offered a rousing and patriotic speech.

Many considered Laborteaux destined for greatness when he

was the first Mead Creek child born in the new century on January 1, 1900. He excelled in sports, played football for the Texas Longhorns, and followed that with law school. He practiced law and kept homes in both Mead Creek and Austin. When only thirty-two years of age, he ran for state representative in the Texas state legislature, and he had held the seat for nearly fifty years.

Like Mayor Stump, Laborteaux showed no signs of slowing down, despite his age.

The Cadillac stopped near the stage as the band finished playing "God Bless America."

Laborteaux opened the door and placed his brown, ostrich boot on the street. He wore green, western-style slacks, a white shirt, and a black bolo tie. He parted his silver-haired mane down the middle. The man was enormous at six foot four and three hundred pounds. He popped his cigar in his mouth and waved with both hands at the few offering polite applause.

"Who's that guy again?" Rut asked.

Wendy shrugged.

"Carlisle Laborteaux," Larry answered. "Some big-time lawyer and politician."

"Yeah, my dad always complains about him," Kevin said. "Said it's guys like him that gave us Jimmy Carter."

Laborteaux stepped up to the microphone.

"Can we boo?" Slade said loudly enough for his parents to hear.

"Hush," his mother scolded.

"Hello, Mead Creek!" Laborteaux bellowed in a deep bass voice. "Thank y'all for coming out on this beautiful evening. I know everyone's ready for fireworks, so I'll be brief."

Laborteaux was known to speak in a slow, Texas drawl while in Mead Creek, but in a quicker, Midwestern accent while in Austin.

"I'm so proud to call Mead Creek my home all these years.

Although we're not in session, we have great things planned in Austin next year. For example . . ."

The speaker droned on as Wendy dropped her face into her hands. "Could this get any more borin'?"

Slade leaned over and spit between his feet. He worked hard to make sure each spit landed on the previous one.

Larry listened in. He scrunched his face not understanding the speaker's joke.

Kevin looked across the street and noticed Ephraim Pollard in front of his hardware store. The street was near dark, but he made out the old man's scowl as Pollard stood with arms crossed. Willie Traynor stood next to him still wearing his green Pollard's Hardware vest. Pollard made several comments out of Kevin's earshot, and Traynor appeared to answer with nods.

Kevin cocked his head and pondered what Pollard might be saying. He seemed so filled with rage.

As Carlisle Laborteaux wrapped up and thanked the crowd, Pollard held out his thumb and index finger. He aimed at Laborteaux and pulled his finger as if firing a gun.

"All right. Fireworks are startin' soon," Rut said.

Kevin elbowed Larry. "You see that?"

"See what?" Larry asked back.

"Old man Pollard. He just pretended to shoot that Laborteaux guy."

Larry looked across the street to see Pollard entering the hardware store. "I didn't see nothin'. What do ya mean?"

"Like that." Kevin mimicked Pollard's finger motion.

Larry replied with a shrug.

A city worker shut off the street lights that had buzzed and illuminated earlier. Shopkeepers turned out their lights as well in anticipation of the fireworks show. Folks chatted up and down the street waiting for dark.

A June bug landed on Kevin's knee. He inched his finger toward it. An instant before his fingertip touched it, it flew away.

Boom!

The first of many rockets exploded in bright colors to the "oohs" and "aahs" of the crowd. The show ended after six minutes with the grand finale and applause.

"You coming home?" Kevin's mother asked him.

"Pretty soon."

She ran her fingers through his hair. "All right, but not too late, understand?"

"Eleven o'clock sharp," Slade's father told his son.

Slade nodded. "Yes, sir."

The parents folded their chairs and headed for their cars.

The five teens had no plans but no reason to go home either.

"What do y'all want to do?" Larry asked.

Rut shrugged.

Kevin stuck his hands in the back pockets of his jean shorts and felt paper. He'd forgotten the gravestone rubbing they'd made that morning from the historical marker. He unfolded and studied it. He looked up at the others. "We were gone so long today we never did look around for this emblem."

"Too late now. Tomorrow," Wendy said. "We should—"

"Hey, guys!" Kim Oberlin walked up holding her husband's hand. "Y'all enjoy the firework show?"

Kevin folded the paper behind his back.

Slade perked up.

"It was okay I guess," Wendy answered.

Mrs. Oberlin tapped her husband's forearm. "This is my husband, David."

"Howdy." He waved.

"These are the ones I told you about, looking into that old Claymore murder."

"Uh-huh. Well, have you found anything interesting?" David asked.

"We met Dickie Claymore. He showed us all kinds of stuff," Rut blurted out.

"Interesting," Kim said. "He usually keeps to himself."

"Yeah, and we thought he was dead," Rut said.

"Dead?" Kim asked.

"Well, yeah," Wendy answered. "We didn't realize anyone even lived there. We've been goin' by all this time thinkin' it was some old haunt . . . I mean . . . empty house."

Kim and David both smiled. "Well, if it's any consolation, a lot of people have made that mistake," David said. "I don't think I've ever met him myself. What's he like?"

"Nice," Kevin said. "Real nice." He looked over his shoulder and lowered his voice. "He took us through his house and told us all about the murders."

Kim leaned in. "Really? How interesting. I would have liked to have been there."

"It was pretty cool," Larry said.

"I guess that murder never will be solved," Kim said.

"Maybe we'll solve it," Kevin announced.

The others shot him a look. That was a secret within the group, and he'd just told an outsider.

Kevin shrugged. "You never know. I mean us . . . or somebody. Someday."

"Well, I hope you do. I'd be happy to help," Kim said.

David tugged her arm down, slightly.

She looked up at him. "Well, we'd better be going. Good luck." They turned and strolled down the sidewalk.

Kevin quickly circled the group. "We should get her to help again. She knows lots of stuff and can help us research all this. Let's ask her."

"I don't know," Larry said.

Rut didn't seem to care.

Slade smiled. "Okay by me."

"I say yes," Wendy said. "We need her."

Larry frowned. "All right."

"Hurry and go ask her," Kevin said to Wendy.

She took off in a jog. "Mrs. Oberlin! Mrs. Oberlin!"

She caught up with the couple as they both turned.

The four boys watched intently as Mrs. Oberlin cocked her head and then nodded.

Wendy jogged back. "She's in!"

The boys nodded in agreement.

"She told us to come by the library in the mornin'," Wendy said.

"We gonna tell her about the shotgun?" Larry asked.

"We have to," Kevin answered. "It might be a key to the investigation."

The others nodded.

"But no parents. They don't need to know anythin' about the shotgun or Dickie or any of that," Kevin said.

More nods.

"Hey there, kiddos!"

Startled, they turned to find Carlisle Laborteaux towering over them. None of them spoke.

He pulled his cigar from his mouth. "Y'all enjoy that fireworks show?"

They nodded and Larry spoke up. "Yes, sir."

He nodded back and moved to the next group of people and

asked, "Y'all enjoy that firework show?"

"Weird," Slade said, looking at the politician. He faced his friends again. "Let's go do somethin'."

"Like what?" Rut asked.

"I dunno," Slade said.

"I'm whooped," Wendy said.

"Me too," Larry said.

"All right, losers. I'll think of somethin' on the way," Slade said.

They retrieved their bikes and headed toward their neighborhood with no plan. That's how most Mead Creek summer days went for teens. But their day had been full. They slow-pedaled and recapped the events of the day. While most their age had spent two dollars in The Oz Arcade, swam at the community pool, or played Monopoly, these five had uncovered a mythical figure. They heard stories most of Mead Creek had never heard. They toured the infamous Claymore mansion. Far from a typical Mead Creek summer day.

⚫◉⚫

DAVID AND KIM Oberlin turned a corner out of downtown toward their apartment.

"You never did tell me how your talk with Pastor J. C. went," Kim said.

"Yeah, I'd been meaning to tell you about that. Kinda weird. He was really dismissive. Basically, said his father is a bitter old man, and that I should leave it alone. Said I ought to pay more attention to the kids playing out in the woods."

Kim stopped and looked at David. "Really? Ephraim must've said something to him. He's really worked up about this."

They continued their walk. The darkness dropped the temperature but the evening was muggy.

David wiped sweat from his forehead. "No offense to old Ephraim, but he's not exactly the type to be worried over the welfare and safety of some local teenagers. What's he really worried about?"

"I think he's just a little freaked out by Dickie Claymore. My grandmother once told me to stay away from the Claymore place. Said Ephraim thought Dickie was dangerous. I wish she were still with us. I have so many questions." Kim looked to the side and pondered. "Oh, well. Guess my day at the library will be a little less boring tomorrow."

"Be careful, Detective. You don't want to incur the wrath of old Ephraim," David said, smiling.

CHAPTER 23

RUT WALKED OUT of his house the next morning, letting the screen door slam shut. He wore a bright red T-shirt with the words "Nanu Nanu," made famous by the show *Mork and Mindy*, on the front.

"What's takin' y'all so long?" Larry asked. He, Kevin, and Slade sat on their bikes in the driveway.

"I was waitin' for that Cars song to come on the radio so I could record it," Rut said. "I like the nightlife, baby," he sang, bobbing his head.

"Wendy?" Kevin asked.

Rut shrugged. "My mom's yellin' at her about somethin'."

The screen door flew open. "I heard you!" Wendy yelled into the house. She reached for her bike, which leaned against the house. "Ugh!" She rolled it toward them. "I hate her!"

"What's goin' on?" Kevin asked.

"Nothin'," she replied and pedaled away.

The rest followed.

Thirty yards later, Wendy answered. "She's impossible. Always tellin' me what to wear. Who I can hang out with. Can't go to the arcade. Ugh!"

The others knew better than to agree with her or reason with her. The mother–daughter relationship during a divorce can be treacherous waters. Few can understand it and certainly not teen boys.

Wendy complained for a solid thirteen minutes until they reached the library.

Kevin had seen her upset before, but never this mad. As they parked their bikes in the rack, he placed a hand on her shoulder. "Sorry. It's gonna be okay."

The simple act disarmed her. Cooled her.

She blew a sigh of relief. "Thanks."

They walked past the front desk as the elderly librarian lifted a skeptical eyebrow.

Kim Oberlin sat with one leg crossed over the other at the microfilm machine. She scrolled as the teens' reflection showed on the screen. She turned. "Well, hello. I was wondering when y'all would show up."

"Her fault." Slade thumbed at Wendy.

"I've been here since early this morning reading. You're just in time because I've found something interesting." Kim turned back to the machine and scrolled through several pages. "Remember that I told you there were other newspaper accounts of the Claymore murders?"

Kevin and Larry nodded.

Wendy took a seat next to her.

"These are from the *Dallas Times Herald*. Nothing unusual in the first few days of coverage. Pretty much the same as the *Mead Creek Daily Register* except the Dallas accounts are a couple of days behind. I guess it took a while to get the new report to their presses. However, about two weeks after the murders, the reporter stated that he'd uncovered new evidence that someone had admitted to the murders." She scrolled forward and pointed to the screen. "This reporter, Randall Crowley. Says here that 'the *Dallas Times Herald* has heard from a witness that will come forward on condition of anonymity to offer evidence of their participation in the incident, but the witness claims that they are not the murderer.'"

"Whoa! That's huge!" Kevin said.

"Yes. Huge!" Mrs. Oberlin replied. "But then, there's this." She scrolled to a few days later. "It's a retraction. This reporter, Crowley, said he regrets that his information was incorrect. And after that, all the other newspaper reports are by someone different. I can't even find a single article from Crowley after that. You know, I've read all these reports but never noticed this before."

"Man, I wish we could talk to him. Probably dead by now."

Mrs. Oberlin crossed her arms. "Just so happens that one of my sorority sisters works at the *Dallas Times Herald*. I called her earlier about him. She'd never heard of him but said she'd do some asking around. Well, she just called me back ten minutes ago. Turns out that Randall Crowley worked at the paper for forty more years but not as a reporter. He did some other job there. That article we read was his final one. She didn't really know why but said a couple of people remember him. Said he was nice and got along with everyone. And, that he's still alive. Lives in a nursing home in Prestonwood."

"Prestonwood. That's like thirty miles from here," Wendy said.

"That's right," Mrs. Oberlin said. "I've already asked for the rest of the day off. As you can see, we're not too busy."

They looked around to find no other patrons visiting the library.

"Who'd like to go with me?" she asked.

"I'm goin'!" Kevin said.

Larry raised a finger. "Me too."

"Okay, but you each have to call and get your parents' permission first," Mrs. Oberlin said.

Slade and Rut whispered. Then Slade spoke up. "I think we're goin' swimmin'. We'll catch you on the way back."

"Seriously! Don't you care?" Larry asked.

Slade shrugged. "Kinda. Just not like every single day."

"Plus, I don't wanna go to no nursin' home," Rut said.

"Suit yourselves." Kevin picked up the receiver on the phone and started dialing.

After Larry and Wendy made their calls, they followed Mrs. Oberlin out the front door.

Kevin whispered to Wendy, "I can't believe your mom is lettin' you go."

"I fake dialed. I just called Time and Temperature," she said.

As Slade and Rut rode off for the community pool, the other three left their bikes and walked to Kim Oberlin's apartment building, where she entered to retrieve her car keys.

They climbed into her 1974 Dodge Dart. The bright green paint had its share of scars, and several cracks inched up the white vinyl top.

As reserved as Mrs. Oberlin had seemed to them, she had no reservations about speeding. She devoted most of her attention to talking about the case and little to driving. Wendy sat in the front and reached for the dash more than once as Kim Oberlin barreled down the highway toward Prestonwood.

Fleetwood Mac's "Go Your Own Way" came on the radio. Mrs. Oberlin reached for the volume and turned it up two notches. "Love this song."

———— • ◉ • ————

A WOMAN IN scrubs rolled a man in his wheelchair through the front door as Mrs. Oberlin, Kevin, Wendy, and Larry passed them and asked for the room of Randall Crowley.

"Mr. Crowley?" The person at the front desk cocked her head. "No one has come to visit him in years." She pointed with her pencil down a long hallway. "Room 118."

"Thank you," Mrs. Oberlin said.

They found the door to room 118 open. A man leaned awkwardly over in his recliner, an open book in his lap, and a rerun of *Leave It to Beaver* played with no sound on the TV. He coughed and cleared his throat.

Mrs. Oberlin knocked on the door. "Excuse me."

He didn't acknowledge.

"I think he's taking a little nap," she whispered. She knocked again. "Excuse me. Are you Randall Crowley?"

He opened his eyes and turned. "What?" He cupped his ear and squinted.

"Are you Mr. Crowley?" Mrs. Oberlin asked.

"Oh. Yep. That's me. Who might you be?"

"I'm Kim Oberlin from Mead Creek. And these are some of my students . . . uh . . . friends. We were hoping to ask you some questions."

"Well, you best come in then. I don't get too many visitors. No family to speak of." He looked around at the lack of chairs. "Find you a spot and park it." He pointed to the bed. "Just move them papers."

The room had few photos or trinkets. Every flat space held a stack of books, magazines, or newspapers. Although the room was a little dusty, the man wore clean clothes and dressed in slacks and a buttoned shirt. He seemed ready for business.

Mrs. Oberlin took the only extra chair, and the three teens sat next to each other on the side of the bed.

He reached forward and turned the TV off. "How do you know who I am?"

"We wanted to ask you about your reporting of the Claymore murders in Mead Creek." Mrs. Oberlin paused for his reaction.

The kids remained quiet and still.

He rubbed his thighs. "You don't say. I haven't thought about that in years. At ninety-four years old, you tend to forget a lot of things." He offered a light snicker but had clearly altered his demeanor.

She continued, "We read you had interviewed a witness or someone admitting to something who then retracted it. Why did they retract?"

"Why are you looking into this?" He scratched his balding head. "So long ago. Why?"

"Because we promised Dickie," Kevin said.

"Who?" Crowley barked.

Kevin looked at his two friends and then back at the elderly man. "Dickie Claymore. We promised him we'd help solve the murder."

"He's still alive?"

"Yes, sir."

Randall Crowley leaned back in his recliner. "That poor little boy. I remember him." He shook his head. "I read he went off to war and was a hero. I assumed he wouldn't live a long life. So much tragedy for him." He leaned over and picked up a pill bottle that sat next to five others. "Doctors say I don't have long to live. Guess I don't have to worry much anymore. Probably should have said something years ago. Too scared I guess."

"Scared of what, sir?" Mrs. Oberlin asked.

"Well, the newspaper sent me down to cover the murders. I was staying at the hotel when someone slipped a piece of paper under my door. I was young and ambitious. It was exciting. The note said to meet them in the alley behind the hotel at 10:30 PM.

"I got there early. I heard footsteps and a voice behind some boxes. The person wouldn't show their face. They told me they knew something about the murders. That he and two others had been near the Claymore mansion that day. He wanted to know if I could protect him if he went to the sheriff. Well, I told him the sheriff would protect him if he was a witness. I tried to get more details from him, but he got worried. Said he had to rethink all of this. Said he'd contact me again in a day or so. Then he just ran off. He seemed kind of young. I could tell he was trying to use a different voice.

"A little older than you kids, though." He pointed at the teens on his bed.

"What happened next?" Wendy asked.

"That's the part I've never told anyone. I wouldn't have even admitted this twenty years ago. Probably would have taken it to the grave had you not shown up. I lied back then and said my source recanted. Was just trying to get their name in the papers. But that's not what happened.

"The next night, I had finished eating dinner and decided to take a walk through town. I stepped off the sidewalk between two buildings when someone grabbed me. I think there were two of them. They threw a hood over my head so I couldn't see anything."

Mrs. Oberlin covered her mouth.

Larry's jaw dropped.

"They dragged me for a bit, off into an alley, punched me, and then threw me on the ground. They said they knew that someone had told me they were a witness. Said the witness didn't see anything and they were wrong. They said if I didn't leave town in the morning that I'd end up just like the Claymores.

"So, I left. I'm ashamed to admit it. But, I was done with that story. My editor was really upset because he thought I'd found a new angle. I told him I didn't want to work in the field anymore. I stayed with the paper but ended up working in the advertising department."

"I guess you don't have any idea who it was that did that?" Mrs. Oberlin asked.

"Nope. Never saw a face. Right before they left, one of them lifted the hood a bit while the other showed me his shotgun. He pumped it, you know, to intimidate me. It was sort of unusual because there was this emblem on the stock, like a Rebel flag."

The three teens spoke no more.

———————— •◉• ————————

THE SHOTGUN AND emblem on the stock meant nothing to Mrs. Oberlin.

As they discussed their visit with the elderly journalist on their drive back, Larry and Kevin whispered a few times.

"Okay," Larry said. "Tell her."

"Mrs. Oberlin. You remember that day we told you about findin' a canteen?" Kevin asked.

"Uh-huh."

Wendy looked over her shoulder at Kevin.

"Well, we really found a shotgun," Kevin said.

Mrs. Oberlin whipped her head around at Kevin. The car swerved across a solid yellow line on the road. She quickly moved back into her lane. She kept her eyes forward and slightly cocked her head. "Let me guess, it had that Pollard's Raiders emblem on the stock, didn't it?" She glanced at Wendy sitting in the passenger seat.

Wendy gave her a single nod. "And we think that Mr. Ephraim heard us talkin' about it by the hardware store. We hid it in a tree, and now it's gone."

"So that's it. It must've been Ephraim Pollard that committed the murders," Kevin stated.

"Yep. Gotta be," Larry said.

"Now hold on. Trust me; I know why you'd think that, but I've seen that emblem since I was a little girl." Mrs. Oberlin looked left through the window. "I've seen it on hats, bumper stickers, cross-stitched and framed. You name it. Plenty of non-Pollards have proudly displayed it. I think you guys have researched this enough to know that many are proud of that group. Even if it's all overblown a bit.

"You guys do realize my grandmother was a Pollard, right?"

"What?" Kevin asked.

"Yep! She was a Pollard. I'm technically a Pollard. Not necessarily the greatest thing to admit, but I guess I should offer that for full disclosure. My grandmother died a few years ago. Her brothers are Mayor Stump and Ephraim. My great uncles. My dad loved his mother but distanced himself from the rest of the Pollard clan. He never liked to talk about them. Still doesn't. My grandmother always said her oldest brother, Ephraim, had an awful temper." She looked over to Wendy and toward the back seat. "Doesn't make him a murderer, though.

"Sometimes I've wanted to dig more into my family history. The famous E. M. Pollard that led the raiders in the Civil War. His son, my great-grandfather, Marshall Pollard, who went to prison. My grandmother didn't have many good things to say about him either. She did speak well of her mother. Said she was respected in the community. Strong businesswoman. Held her own against the men in town in the days when women couldn't even vote. She turned a little general store into the hardware and lumber business it is today.

"It's weird, though. Some family members like to talk about Pollard family history, but others shut you down. My husband says some people don't like to open up old family wounds."

They passed the "Welcome to Mead Creek" sign on the highway. Larry and Kevin looked to their left at the entrance to Devil's Backbone.

Mrs. Oberlin turned just short of Main Street, and they passed between the First Baptist Church and the city swimming pool.

"There's Slade and Rut," Wendy said.

The car pulled up next to them and slowed to a stop.

Both had wet, moppy hair and drenched cutoffs.

Kevin grabbed the window handle and cranked it down. "What's up?"

Rut lifted his head for a hello.

Slade shrugged. "Just swimmin'. Y'all find out anythin' interestin'?"

"Oh, yeah. We have a lot to tell you," Kevin answered.

CHAPTER 24

AFTER DROPPING THE kids off at the library so they could retrieve their bicycles, Mrs. Oberlin decided to share the day's events with her husband and headed for the church. Halfway there, she made a U-turn for the sheriff's office.

She approached the secretary, who brushed Liquid Paper across a page inserted in her typewriter. "Is the sheriff in?"

"Oh, real busy," she said, sarcastically, with a wink. "Go ahead." She motioned with her head for Kim Oberlin to see the sheriff.

With his two deputies making after-lunch rounds, Sheriff Raymond Traynor sat behind his desk, fiddling with a fishing rod and reel. He smoothed his hair, which was thick on the back of his head but absent on top. The light glared off his skull. He was competent, caring, and serious about his role of protecting Mead Creek. He knew that many looked down on his father, Willie Traynor, who never made it beyond a hardware store clerk. He defended his father and would tell his two sons that their grandfather was the epitome of putting in a hard day's work.

She knocked on the open door.

"Well, hey there, young lady."

"Got a minute?"

"Sure." He stood and pointed to the open chair in front of his desk. "Have a seat." He reached back and worked the cords to open the blinds for a little more light. "So, what's going on?" he said, taking his seat.

"Well, I'm not quite sure where to start, but I want to bounce something off you." She proceeded to lay out the Claymore murder case, how the teens had revived her interest, their experiences with Dickie, and the now missing shotgun. "So, as you can see, this might really mean something."

Sheriff Traynor chuckled. "Well, that's one helluva story." He folded his arms and rested them on his paunch. "Look, darling. This is just like every November; someone says they know who killed JFK. Every ten years or so, some hotshots play detective and come here telling me they can solve the case. They always say, 'I got new evidence.'"

Kim moved to the edge of her seat. "New evidence? Like a witness claiming they were intimidated? The potential murder weapon found and then stolen? The way Ephraim Pollard has been acting? Are you telling me that's not compelling?"

"Well, now, cool down." He stroked his bushy mustache. "Isn't ole Ephraim your uncle?"

"Great uncle. Yes. And I'm not saying he's guilty. Innocent until proven guilty. I believe in that." Kim measured her words.

He stood, hinting for her to leave. "Tell ya what. I'll look into the matter. Good enough?"

Mrs. Oberlin knew she was being dismissed, but she had no other options. As she reached the doorway, she glanced back. "Look, Sheriff. I know how crazy all this sounds. And I'm well aware of what it means to go up against the establishment. And in this town, it's the Pollards."

He remained standing. "Little lady, you're wise beyond your

years."

———————————•◉•———————————

THE TEENS GROUPED their bikes on the edge of the downtown square for a strategy session.

Kevin showed the gravestone rubbing of the Pollard's Raiders emblem.

"I don't get it," Slade said. "What are we lookin' for?"

"Let's see who all has the emblem. Like on their wall or somethin'. They might know who would have that on a shotgun," Kevin said.

"Yeah, but it was like a hundred years ago. They won't know anythin'," Rut said.

"Really?" Kevin pointed to the other end of town at the Dairy Queen. "You remember all those stories we heard? Remember how much Dickie has told us? Think about how mad that Ephraim Pollard was at us about it. It's like the biggest thing that happened in this town. People want to remember. It's why there's a historical marker out there."

"He's right," Wendy said. "We'll split up. Me and Kevin will take this side and you three stooges take that side." She smirked.

"Spread out!" Kevin said, in his best Moe voice.

"You know, you say a lot of crap that would normally get your butt kicked if you weren't a girl," Slade said to Wendy.

She raised her fists. "Put your dukes up, tough guy."

They all laughed knowing she was kidding.

Except for Rut. He shook his head and rolled his eyes. "Why does she get away with that crap?"

"Dude. She's a girl. It's the way the world works." Kevin was elated she chose him for this next, although mild, adventure.

Each group worked their way down the street. Walking their

bikes, parking them, entering stores and businesses.

Kevin and Wendy made Pollard's Hardware their next location.

A child whined to his mother for one more ride on the coin-operated horse in front of the store.

Wendy cupped her hands around her face and peered through the window. "I don't see that old dude. Let's go in."

They entered cautiously, nearly arm in arm. This was not too different than entering the rear of the Claymore mansion, though they had a little less fear.

A lady with a gray, beehive hairstyle shooting up from her head rang the cash register and handed change to a customer. "Eight, nine, and that makes ten. You be sure and tell Gladys I said hello, now."

A few other patrons browsed the aisles as an AM station played "Green, Green Grass of Home."

Modern shelving lined the aisles, but sprinkled throughout were relics from the past. A rusted plow and other antiques hung from the ceiling or sat atop cabinets. A sign next to the cash register read: In God We Trust. All Others Pay Cash.

A nine-point buck with glistening eyes was mounted. Kevin imagined it said, "What do you think you're doing in here?"

They walked to the back end of the store, earning a few stares from those that were there for business.

I wonder if they know what we're doing, Kevin thought. He twirled a spinning display rack that held dozens of different nails and screws.

As they returned to the front, Kevin paused and pulled on Wendy's arm to stop.

She mouthed, "What?"

He pointed over the beehived hair.

How they missed it on their first walk-through remained a

mystery. Nicely framed was a worn and tattered flag identical to the symbol on the historical marker and the emblem on the shotgun. This one, however, was huge, with color. The background was blood red. The blue bars had faded to a dull gray, and the white stars had yellowed. The name "Pollard's Raiders" was sewn in, with "Pollard's" curved down and "Raiders" curved up to form a circle. The letter C, for cavalry, was on the left and "6th," for 6th Regiment, on the right. The frayed edges offered even more character, although the modern, metal frame seemed awkward.

Wendy slowly cocked her head and studied it.

It frightened Kevin.

"Pretty neat, huh?"

Kevin shivered at the abrupt voice.

Wendy clutched her chest.

Willie Traynor stood behind them with hands on hips. He wiped sweat from his brow with his arm and gave a welcoming smile. His teeth looked to have never met a dentist.

"Well, what d'ya think of it?" he asked, pointing at the flag.

Kevin shrugged. "Pretty cool, I guess." He noticed the logo on Traynor's green vest had Pollard's Hardware arched in the same manner as the Pollard's Raiders on the flag.

Traynor scoffed. "Cool? Don't you kids know what that flag is from?"

Wendy shook her head, playing dumb.

"Why, that's from the Battle of Mead Creek. The owner of this here store, Ephraim Pollard, well, his granddaddy led the Raiders. They attacked the Yankees out near the creek before they could ambush this town. They whooped 'em good. Saved this town from God-knows-what. They're heroes. Every last one of 'em. I met a few of them fellers when I was your age. They'd be in this here store sittin' right there playin' cards."

He pointed to a table and three chairs in the corner across from the cashier. Newspapers, an ashtray with several stubbed-out cigarettes, and an empty coffee cup sat atop the table. Ephraim Pollard occasionally invited guests and spent many mornings there discussing days of old as well as current events.

"Instead of that table, there'd be a barrel for the cards and four chairs. They'd tell some of the best stories you ever heard. Like this one time, they—"

"Hey, Willie, how about helpin' Mrs. Welch out with her bags?" the cashier asked before she began reminding another customer what items were on sale.

He held up a finger. "Be right there."

Kevin rubbed his chin, a move typically reserved for an older detective. "I guess we do know a little bit about it. Like how that flag is the emblem on the historical marker out on the highway."

"Why, sure," Traynor smiled. "Folks have that on lots of things. They're awful proud of it."

"Like on the barrel of a shotgun?" Kevin asked.

Wendy's eyes widened.

Traynor's did as well. "I . . . I don't know what you're talkin' about. I have to get back to work." He stepped aside and began bagging Mrs. Welch's purchases. He looked over at Kevin and Wendy but quickly looked away.

"That was weird," Wendy whispered to Kevin.

Kevin nodded. "Let's get outta here."

They jumped on their bikes and rode toward their friends across Main Street. Kevin updated them on their meeting as he and Willie Traynor kept trading glances while he loaded bags in the trunk of Mrs. Welch's Lincoln Continental.

Traynor rubbed his face as he made a hurried entrance into the hardware store.

"Y'all find anythin'?" Wendy asked.

"Yep. The cafe had the emblem on a plaque by all those other ones they have in the entryway," Larry said.

"Did you ask anybody about it?" Kevin asked.

"Nope." Slade straddled his bike and folded his arms. "The waitress kicked us out."

"Why did she kick y'all out?"

"'No shirts. No shoes. No service,' she said."

Kevin scrunched his eyes. "But, you're wearin' shirts and shoes."

"No money," Slade said. "That's what she really meant."

"Doesn't matter. I'm convinced now that Mr. Pollard's the killer." Kevin slapped the back of one open hand into the other. "You could tell the way that Willie Traynor guy acted when I brought up the shotgun. He knows. I think Ephraim Pollard killed the Claymores, buried the shotgun, and that Traynor is coverin' for him. He was actin' so proud of Pollard's Raiders but not when I brought up the emblem on the shotgun.

"We gotta go tell Dickie!"

"Wait. What if you're wrong?" Larry asked. "He's been through so much. We don't wanna upset him."

"We can't tell Mrs. Oberlin any more," Rut said. "Y'all said she's a Pollard. Probably coverin' up for 'em too."

"Shut up, Rut! She's not like that," Wendy said.

Rut scoffed.

"I have an idea," Larry said. "Let's tell those guys at Dairy Queen."

"Then the whole town will know," Slade said.

Larry gave Slade a single nod. "Exactly. Why keep it a secret anymore? Nobody's gonna believe us. But if a bunch of grown-ups come forward, maybe tell the sheriff, somethin' will get done about it."

•◆•

THE DAIRY QUEEN was oddly empty of elderly men slapping cards. Three sat at their usual table sipping coffee. Dickie's child-hood friend, Frank, the hard-of-hearing Jesse, and a man they'd not seen before.

Kevin approached the table.

Frank looked up. "Well, I was wonderin' if you kids were ever comin' back."

"We kinda have somethin' important to tell you about Dickie. Kinda private."

Frank looked at their friend. "Say, Al. You wanna excuse us a minute? Got important business with our friends." Frank winked at Al.

Al looked at the kids. He nodded at Frank. "Well, I was about to be gettin' anyhow."

The five teens pulled up chairs and surrounded Frank and Jesse.

"I'm afraid Bill had a date with his favorite fishin' hole, so he's not here today," Frank said.

"Any of you Pollards?" Rut asked.

"Nope. Not me," Frank said. He raised his voice. "Jesse, you a Pollard?"

"Hell, no!" Jesse answered.

Kevin updated them on their time spent with Dickie, the missing shotgun, their latest findings, and their belief that Ephraim Pollard murdered the Claymore family.

"I've seen that shotgun," Jesse said. "A bunch of them Pollard's Raiders gave it to their commander, E. M. Pollard. Kind of a trophy. They used to have a reunion every five years or so. This was about nineteen and five best I can remember. I was a little kid then and

Major Pollard was an old man. Kinda like me now. He was too frail to even shoot the darn thing.

"They had this parade in town where all the raiders walked down the street. Only seven or eight of 'em by then. My pa made sure I knew who was who and what was what. Pollard's Raiders this and that, ya know. I remember it because E. M. Pollard died the next day. They found him on his front porch with the shotgun between his legs."

Slade leaned forward in his chair. "Whoa. He killed himself?"

"Nah," Jesse answered. "Old age. Old fellers like us keel over all the time. I might die while I'm sitting here talking to ya."

The teens sat with no expression.

Rut looked more in shock.

Jesse burst out laughing.

"Y'all 'scuse ole Jesse. He likes to tease," Frank said. "Why don't you get back to the shotgun, Jesse?"

"All right. My pa did business with Marshall Pollard. That's E. M.'s son. Marshall was the father of Ephraim and Mayor Stump. Marshall told my pa that he had the shotgun and planned to pass it down to his oldest. Well, that'd be Ephraim. When Marshall got sent away to prison, Ephraim was probably fourteen or fifteen. That's when he probably got the—"

Jesse stopped and cupped his hand over his mouth. His light-hearted demeanor tapered off.

"I think I know what Jesse is thinkin', but he doesn't wanna say it," Frank said.

Jesse nodded at Frank.

"You kids remember we told you how Dickie's father was the prosecutor in these parts?" Frank asked.

Kevin and Larry nodded.

"Well, remember he was the one that put Ephraim's dad in

prison. I mean, the judge did it, but Richard Claymore pushed for it."

Jesse lowered his hand. "All these years, I never thought this through. When you're a prosecutor, you might have plenty of fellers out for you. But no one ever thought it'd be someone like Ephraim. He was a mean kid, but still a kid."

"Fifteen was pretty much a grown-up back in them days," Frank said.

Jesse cocked his head. "I reckon that's true. There's another possibility."

"What?" Frank asked.

Jesse tapped his finger on the table. "The Raiders did it."

Frank scoffed.

"I mean to tell ya," Jesse said.

"What do you mean the Raiders did it?" Kevin asked Jesse.

Frank answered, "You kids know what the Ku Klux Klan is?"

"You mean like on that television program *Roots*?" Rut asked.

The bell on the door clanked as a family of four came in and ordered.

"Yeah, that's it," Frank answered. "Well, when I was a kid, there were rumors that the Pollard's Raiders used to ride around after the Civil War. Not so much like the KKK, burnin' crosses and such, but just sort of like a rightin' of what they thought were wrongs. Like we didn't need no sheriff because the Raiders would take care of things.

"Well, they weren't all that secret. I mean, if you was a Raider, you told everyone you was a Raider. You was proud of it. Some folks hoped that their sons, or other guys they recruited, would keep the Raiders goin'. One time when I was in school, this one kid said if these other fellers didn't quit pickin' on him, the Raiders would come after them. You see, it was stuff like that. Nothin' real as far as folks could tell. Just rumors."

"What if the Raiders were still around?" Kevin asked.

"I don't think so," Frank said. "That rumor died out a long time ago. Only those with an overactive imagination like Jesse here still believe it."

Jesse swatted at Frank.

"Y'all know the high school principal, Mr. Self? His granddaddy was the last of the original Raiders to die. Was only fourteen in the fight. Rode with his father. Lived until just after World War II. He was the last one. Real nice feller. He wouldn't've been caught up in nothin' illegal. Churchgoing feller. Straight as they come. Just like his grandson the principal.

"Listen, kids. At first, I thought y'all was just lettin' your imagination run away with ya, like them ghost stories. But, you may be onto somethin'. I think the sheriff ought to know. Your parents know any—"

"Oh, my lands!" one of the DQ workers shouted as she finished taking a family's order.

"What on earth, Esther?" Frank said to her.

She thumbed toward the mom of the family. "They just told me there was a terrible car accident on the other side of town. A car ran right off the road into a telephone pole. Some young lady. They're taking her to the hospital in Cranville. Looks serious."

The customer that had brought the news sipped from her straw, then looked at Frank, Jesse, and the teens. "Poor thing. That sweet girl that works at the library. Kim Ober-something."

CHAPTER 25

THE FORT OFFERED the five teens some thinking space. They had thanked Frank and Jesse for their time but told them they'd tell their parents later because they wanted to be sure. Frank and Jesse replied with a "suit yourself" attitude and let the teens be on their way. They wasted no time in leaving Dairy Queen, rolled straight past Dickie's house, and entered the fort.

It was a scorcher. August in Texas can be unbearable, but July isn't much different. The fort baked them like an oven, but they chose its protection. When first constructed, the fort could have been knocked over by a swift kick, but Dickie's work had made it sturdy. However, it wasn't a real fort. It wouldn't protect them from unseen forces or Pollard's Raiders or any physical attack. They loved its secrecy, in that only the five, plus Dickie, knew about it.

"Poor Mrs. Oberlin. Wonder what happened," Wendy said.

Slade lifted his shirt to wipe the sweat from his face. "Where was she goin' when she dropped y'all off anyway?"

Wendy shrugged.

"Man. Hope she'll be okay," Larry said.

Kevin shook his head slowly. "We gotta do somethin'," he announced. "I mean I care about Mrs. Oberlin, hope she's okay and all, but we can't wait for her. We have to figure all this out. Who all is involved. We have to solve this ourselves. But we have to be careful. Pollard's Raiders still exist. They might be all over town."

Wendy nodded. "Yep. No doubt about it."

"We don't know that. Might just be a bunch of rumors," Larry said. "What do you think, Slade?"

He shrugged. "Dunno. The whole dang thing is fishy if you ask me. That old dude—what's his name?—Jesse. He's been around forever. He oughta know."

Rut stood and stuck his face by an opening, hoping to catch a breeze. "I don't know why we came all the way out here. We should just tell the sheriff. He'll know what to do."

"'Cuz, this is where it's safe. Nobody knows about this place. We need time to think."

The back and forth and rehashing of events continued for an hour.

"Maybe we should get my dad," Slade suggested.

Kevin scoffed. "He won't believe us. He'll say we're makin' it all up."

"Yeah. That's a waste of time," Larry said. "If we say anythin' to anybody, and I mean if, it should be the sheriff."

They all looked at each other and nodded.

"Is this the part where we spit in our hands and shake?" Slade said, with a chuckle.

Rut snorted in and fake-spit in his palm, pretending to fill it with nastiness. He extended his hand toward Wendy.

"Gross! What a pig," Wendy said.

Rut smiled.

"Okay, then. I guess we should go back to town," Kevin said.

"What about tellin' Dickie?" Wendy asked.

Larry shook his head. "Nope. Still don't think we should. Don't want him to be disappointed. We might be wrong about all this."

They exited the fort and began picking up their bikes.

Larry walked toward the creek. "I'll catch up. Gonna stick my head in and cool off."

The other four walked their bikes through the short, but thick trail to the opening near Meyer's Pond. As they emerged, Sheriff Traynor leaned on his two-tone police car, smiling.

The sedan, with dark brown coloring except for the white front doors, was well known in town. On rare occasions, the lights and siren would go off, typically for an out-of-town speeder. Dirt covered the fenders and tires from a rough trip down Devil's Backbone.

The sheriff wore a standard uniform although his shirt buttons struggled over his belly from a "six pack of beer after supper" habit. His belt held a .38 Colt revolver with wood grips. He crossed his arms. "Well, hey there, kids. We've been looking for you."

Rut swallowed hard. "Holy crapamoly!"

"Lookin' for us?" Kevin whispered, questioning the remark. He saw the unmistakable fedora through the backseat window.

Ephraim Pollard turned his head, looked at the four teens, and used one hand to rub his unshaven face. His window was cracked three inches.

The passenger door opened as a large man stepped out. The right side of the car sprang up in relief from the three hundred pounds exiting. Carlisle Laborteaux walked around the front of the vehicle and leaned against the hood next to the sheriff. The car succumbed once again to his weight. His clothes and boots were similar to those he wore at the parade, but this time he had dressed in brown slacks. "How y'all doing?"

Wendy shrugged.

"Ya been lookin' for us?" Kevin asked.

Rut backed his bike a few steps, seeking protection away from the frontline. Kevin, Wendy, and Slade stood their ground, but all were scared.

The sheriff pushed up and took two steps toward them, now standing twenty feet away. "There was a bit of an accident in town a few hours ago. That librarian, Kim Oberlin, drove off the road and into a telephone pole. Poor girl. Damn shame. Should be more careful, though. Some folks said y'all was with her. So, we just wanted to make sure you were safe and all."

Kevin shrugged. "We're fine." He began to move his bike to leave the scene.

The other three followed suit.

"Now, hold up just a minute. I ain't through with ya," Traynor said.

They stopped.

"I hear you kids found something out here." Laborteaux spoke with a commanding voice, rarely challenged by opposing politicians, and certainly not about to be challenged by four teenagers. "Well. Did ya?"

"A bullet!" Rut blurted out.

Slade looked at him, disbelief on his face. "A bullet," he mouthed.

Rut shrugged.

Laborteaux chuckled. "Well, that might be, but I'm talking about something a little bigger. Say, a shotgun?"

Pollard had yet to exit the car.

"Might as well admit it. They know," Wendy whispered.

"Yep. We found a shotgun. Back there." Kevin thumbed in the direction of the fort. "But it's gone now." He pointed at Pollard. "And we think he stole it."

Pollard whipped his head toward the teens. He opened the door and hopped out, moving well for his age. "What the hell you say, boy?"

Kevin dropped his bike and pointed at him. "You stole our shotgun. We had it hidden in a hollowed-out tree. You heard us talkin' about it that day by your store. And you came out here and stole it." Kevin had crossed a line. He'd not only issued a huge accusation but also confronted the sheriff and the two most powerful men in Mead Creek.

Pollard ripped off his fedora. "That's a bald-faced lie. You oughta have your hide tanned for sayin' such a lie."

Laborteaux swatted at Pollard. "Cool down, now, Ephraim." He looked at the teens and smiled. He dropped his Texas drawl for a more educated, lawyerly speech. "Now, listen here, kids. We've established you found a shotgun buried out here. Mr. Pollard has admitted he heard you talking about it and the emblem you saw. I think we're all discussing the same shotgun."

"You see, that's a family heirloom. So Mr. Pollard just wants to get back what's rightly his."

"So why was it buried out here?" Wendy asked, in an accusing tone.

"Lost it huntin'. Years ago. Doesn't matter. It's mine, and I want it back," Pollard said.

Slade leaned toward Kevin and whispered through the side of his mouth. "How do you lose a shotgun huntin'?"

Kevin nodded.

Laborteaux pushed himself up from the car and placed his hands on his hips. He walked several steps, reaching the shade of a tree. He looked at Sheriff Traynor. "It's too dang hot out here for all this back and forth. Let me cut to the chase."

Traynor nodded.

Pollard sat back inside the running car, seeking relief from the air conditioner, but kept the window cracked to listen in.

Laborteaux reached up to a branch and pulled off a handful of leaves. He fidgeted with them and tore one to pieces. "You don't get to my age and position without staying one step ahead of the next guy. I know you kids have been running around town with some wild story about the Claymore murders. You even think Mr. Pollard there had something to do with it. That's a pretty serious accusation. Some folks might even say it's a crime to falsely accuse someone like that. You might get thrown in jail for saying something like that." He looked directly at Kevin.

"Oh, crap. Oh, crap," Rut whispered.

He threw down the rest of the leaves and took three angry steps toward them. He pointed at Kevin's chest. "Now I want you to stop this. I better not hear you say another word about any of this. Or else."

Kevin crossed his arms. "Or else what?"

—— • ◉ • ——

LARRY HAD HEARD every word but remained concealed behind thick greenery. He didn't have Kevin's passion for the investigation but had watched enough detective shows with his father to realize innocent people don't drive down a rough dirt road in the hundred-degree heat to confront a bunch of teenagers.

I gotta tell someone, he thought.

Larry tiptoed while carrying his bike toward the fort. He had raised the bike over his shoulders and moved along the creek bed as fast as he could. He found an opening to reach Devil's Backbone far enough down that the adults wouldn't see him. He mounted his bike, took one look back at his friends, then pedaled down the road in a fury.

He approached the bend toward the Claymore mansion but planned to go straight into town. Dickie was one old man against two other old men and the sheriff. The closest other adults were at Pollard's Lumber, but they would side with Ephraim Pollard. Dairy Queen was the goal.

He rounded the road, avoided the dip he knew was coming just before the cemetery gate. He rose up and pedaled hard, looking toward the Claymore mansion.

Three men stood next to a brown truck with a camper attached, talking with Dickie.

In the many trips past the home, Larry had never seen visitors. He slammed on his brakes as dirt flew from his tires. It was the old men from Dairy Queen.

Frank turned and yelled, "Hey there, son. You best c'mere."

———— •◉• ————

DAVID OBERLIN SAT next to his wife's bed, head in his hands, at Cranville Memorial Hospital. She remained unconscious with a tube down her throat. One eye was blackened and both arms were bruised.

She opened the good eye. "Where am I?"

David looked up and reached for her hand. "You were in an accident."

A doctor walked in, thumbing through papers on a blue plastic clipboard, followed by Pastor J. C. Pollard.

"I'm Doctor Samuel. That was quite an accident. I've looked at her X-rays and tests and can tell you surgery won't be needed. She's got a few broken ribs, but no concussion or head injury."

She closed her eyes and fell back to sleep.

"We have her on some heavy medications. She may be in and out. She needs to rest. I think she'll be just fine." He walked out.

"Thank God," Pastor J. C. said.

Kim opened her eyes again.

"What happened? Do you remember anything?" her husband asked.

She opened her mouth but spoke in such a low whisper, neither of them could hear.

David lowered his ear to her mouth.

"The sheriff," she said.

CHAPTER 26

THE FOUR OLD men talked under the shade of a tree.

Jesse lowered the tailgate and sat. "Phew. I'm plumb worn out from the ride out here. Dadgum, Dickie. Why don't you get that road fixed? Maybe you'd get more visitors."

"Maybe that's the idea," Dickie answered.

Vehicles could only travel a few miles per hour down the rough terrain of Devil's Backbone.

"What brings you out here?" Dickie asked.

Frank and Bill looked at one another.

"You might as well be the one to tell him since you heard it," Bill said.

"I s'pose," Frank said. "Listen, Dickie. This may sound crazy, but you know them kids that have been runnin' around your place and visitin' with ya?"

Dickie nodded.

"Well, they been kinda comin' to visit us as well, over at the DQ. They came today and talked with me and that old codger." Frank thumbed toward Jesse.

"What'd you say, Frank?" Jesse asked, cupping his ear.

Frank shook his head in disgust. "What they told us was so

crazy, we went and got Bill to sorta talk about it. We thought we should go to the sheriff, but—"

Bill sliced his hand through the air with authority. "But I told 'em 'no.' See, I think the sheriff is part of this whole thing."

"You ain't even told him what's what," Jesse said.

"I'm gettin' to that now," Frank said. "You see, Dickie. We think them kids have solved your family's murder. And I know you've heard that before. But, this is different."

Dickie slowly removed his worn and dirty ball cap. "That can't be."

Frank, Bill, and Jesse took turns relating the teens' findings, their theory, and the conspiracy they thought might be at work.

Frank placed a hand on his shoulder. "I know this all sounds crazy."

"And, ya see, reason we didn't go to the sheriff is that I think he might be in with them Pollards," Bill said. "I'd go fishing on occasion with Willie Traynor. His son came with us, maybe eight, ten years ago before he was sheriff, just a deputy. He started going on and on about Pollard's Raiders, their heroics in the war—ya know, all that stuff—and then went on some crazy rant about how the Raiders are still alive in the hearts and minds of Mead Creek citizens. His daddy, Willie, reminded him that no Traynor was a Raider. He got awful mad and said a Raider ain't just about blood, but about believing in the cause."

Dickie took a seat next to Jesse on the tailgate. "I've had so many tell me they were going to solve the case. They were just so sure. But I learned a long time ago to not get excited—this is the first time in decades that I believe it. Because I've always thought Ephraim Pollard had something to do with this.

"The Pollards hated my daddy for their father's conviction. They claimed he died in prison on account of my daddy. I remember

Ephraim, his mom, and his brother staring at us when we'd go to town. You could feel the hate. I'd ask my daddy what was wrong with them. He'd say, 'Their father did a terrible thing, but they blame me for the consequences.'"

"You always said you saw three fellers running away after the murders. That right?" Bill asked.

Dickie nodded. "That's right. Never saw their faces. I've always wondered if it was Ephraim, his brother, and one of their friends."

"Traynor!" Frank said. "Much as I hate to say it, Willie Traynor stuck to them Pollard boys like a leech. He might've been with them."

"Willie Traynor wouldn't swat a mosquito if it was biting on his neck," Bill said.

"Don't mean he weren't with 'em," Frank replied. "If only we had that shotgun. That's gotta be some kind of proof."

"I've got it," Dickie said. "I was out there fixing up the kids' fort. I was afraid it would cave in on them. I found the shotgun. As soon as I saw the emblem, I thought it might be the one used in the murders. Why else would that shotgun be out in the woods like that? No offense to those kids, but I wanted to put it somewhere safe. I planned on telling them but just hadn't gotten around to it."

Jesse fanned himself with his straw fedora. "Well, what we gonna do about it? Before I keel over and die, that is. I'm eighty-four years old, and y'all done drug me out in the middle of nowhere."

"We could call the sheriff in Cranville," Bill suggested.

Frank shook his head. "Nah, he probably knows Sheriff Traynor pretty good. We should call someone in Dallas. Maybe the police there. Let's go inside and use your phone, Dickie."

"I don't have a phone. Somebody might call the darn thing."

"Well, we better head back to town, or I'm gonna have to get my nap," Jesse said.

"Hey, there's one of them kids now on his bike," Frank said. "Hey there, son. You best c'mere!"

Larry rode quickly toward the house, stopped, and remained seated on his bike.

"Where are your friends?" Frank asked.

Larry breathed hard. "They're . . . they're—"

"Take your time, son," Dickie said.

Larry took in a deep breath, released it, and pointed in the direction of the fort. "Back there. The sheriff, that Laborteaux man, and Ephraim Pollard are talkin' to my friends. Kinda yellin' at them."

"That's why I've never voted for that Laborteaux son of a gun," Jesse said.

Larry explained how he had managed to avoid the altercation and shared his version of recent events.

"We gotta get down there!" Frank said. "No time for the law to get here from some other place."

"Us?" Bill said. "We're just a bunch of old men. Hell, Jesse there hardly survived the ride out here."

"We're going down there. But we're not going empty-handed," Dickie said.

———— •◉• ————

KEVIN WAS NO perfect teenager. He didn't like to lie and would never steal. His parents thought him a model child, but the devil on his left shoulder sometimes won out over the angel on the right. His father demanded he respect authorities, such as teachers, coaches, or the Oz that ran the arcade. Carlisle Laborteaux certainly was one of those authorities. But he'd challenged Kevin's passion for solving the murder case.

Why is he protecting Ephraim Pollard? Kevin thought.

"Why does this matter to you so much anyway?" Slade asked.

Kevin stood his ground. "My dad always says, 'If you see a wrong, do your best to right it.'"

Laborteaux came out from the shade taking two giant steps toward them. The temperature approached triple digits. Sweat soaked his shirt, and he wasn't pleased with Kevin's defiance. "Listen here, you little shit. Nobody speaks to me like that. Sure not some little snot-nosed kid. I'll have all four of you arrested. Ain't that right, Sheriff?"

The sheriff stepped forward and unsnapped his holster. "That's right. And you know what happens to some people when they go to jail? They never come out the same."

Rut grabbed Wendy's hand.

She took it.

Slade stepped up and whispered in Kevin's ear. "Dude, forget this. Just tell 'em we were wrong and let's go."

Kevin looked at his three friends. "Can't do it. It's for Dickie. And his family."

<hr />

THE MOTLEY GROUP of old men rolled and dipped down Devil's Backbone at a glacial pace. Frank drove with Bill on the passenger side and Jesse in the middle. They dropped off Dickie and Larry a hundred yards away from the fort.

"Dadburnit, this road's gonna kill me," Jesse complained.

"We could've left you in the hammock under the shade tree at Dickie's," Frank said.

"No, sir. I'm going out of this world in a shootout," Jesse said. "Like Wyatt Earp."

Bill rolled down his window and spit tobacco juice. "Wyatt Earp died from a urinary tract infection. Probably the same thing that'll kill you. Besides, it ain't gonna come to no shootout. Don't know why Dickie gave us this shotgun. Hell, Jesse, you ain't even strong enough to shoot. Remember: Stick to the story. We're just out here fishing, headed to Meyer's Pond."

•◆•

"THEY'RE ON THE road between the pond and the fort, right?" Dickie asked Larry.

"Yes, sir!"

Larry followed Dickie down a trail running parallel to Devil's Backbone.

"Ain't never been down this way," Larry said.

"There are dozens of these trails, and I know every one of them." Dickie pushed brush aside and moved with stealth—crossbow in hand. He switched to a whisper, "I don't like having you involved in this, but I don't want to leave you alone near the house or on the way to town. I have no idea what we're headed for."

Larry stayed on his tail and ignored the pain of thorns slapping his shins. "This like the war, Dickie?"

"Other than missing the threat of mustard gas, and Germans shooting at me, it's a little like it. We have to treat this just like battle."

"You gonna shoot 'em with that bow?"

Dickie shrugged and whispered, "Hope I don't need to, young man. I'm hoping the sheriff and those other two come driving by any minute on the way out of here. Pass by Frank and Bill with nothing more than a wave. Or maybe they head out the other way past the pond. Not much road that way, though. I'm hoping we find your friends by the fort, unharmed."

Crunch!

"Whoops," Larry mouthed after stepping on a branch.

Dickie stopped. "That's okay. Just watch your steps. Let your footfalls come down easy. One eye on where you'll place your feet and the other eye looking ahead."

They moved as fast as Bill's truck and noticed the sheriff's car through the brush.

Dickie held up a hand signaling Larry to stop. "Listen, if anything happens to me, the shotgun you found is in the secret passage. You know where I'm talking about, right?"

Larry nodded.

* * *

KEVIN TURNED TO his friends and whispered, "Listen! I'm gonna distract them and y'all take off the back way. Carry your bikes across the creek and then ride fast. They're old men. They won't catch you."

"Whatchya talkin' 'bout over there?" Sheriff Traynor barked.

"Settle down there, Sheriff," Laborteaux said, swatting his hand. "I think these youngins are coming to their senses."

"We can't leave ya here," Wendy whispered back.

"No way," Slade said. "We ain't leavin' ya."

Rut shrugged.

The rumble of Bill's truck and the squeak from his suspension attracted the attention of both parties.

Sheriff Traynor snapped his holster closed.

No one spoke, and all turned as the truck approached, dipped, and rolled to a stop.

Kevin smiled. "It's Frank, ole Jesse, and that other guy, Bill."

Laborteaux returned to the shade of the tree and offered a patronizing wave.

Pollard stepped out from the comfort of the air-conditioned car.

They stopped behind the sheriff's car, as Devil's Backbone was barely one lane wide.

Frank, in the passenger seat, rolled down the window. "Howdy!" He kept the double-barreled shotgun concealed between his right leg and the door with the tip of the barrel resting on the floorboard.

"How y'all doing?" Laborteaux asked. "Y'all lost or something?"

"No more lost than you!" Jesse said with an authoritative nod.

Bill elbowed him. "Simmer down."

"What'd he say?" Sheriff Traynor asked.

"Nothin'," Frank answered. "He just means we're tryin' to find that fishin' hole. Ain't been down here in years."

"Fishing, huh?" Again, Laborteaux grabbed a twig and picked at the leaves.

The sheriff and Pollard positioned themselves next to Laborteaux under the shade tree, forming a barrier between the four teens and three old men.

"Ephraim," Frank said, with a polite nod.

Pollard returned the nod. "Frank."

Bill gave a wave.

Jesse folded his arms and looked straight ahead.

Rut whispered, "Okay. Let's make a run for it."

Slade leaned over and curled his lip. "Be cool, Rut."

CHAPTER 27

"WHAT ARE Y'ALL doin' out here on such a hot day?" Frank asked.

"Trespassers!" Sheriff Traynor said. "We got a call from folks complaining about some teenagers trespassing out here."

Frank smirked. "Trespassin'? Who the hell cares about trespassin' out here? The only person that owns property out here is old Dickie. Who complained?"

"Well, that's police business. Doesn't concern you none," Traynor said. "Y'all best just turn around. Ain't no fishing out here anyhow. Nobody's caught anything in Meyer's Pond since the drought of '57. We'll deal with these kids." The sheriff thumbed over his shoulder in the direction of the four teens.

Frank moved his head to the left and right, looking around Laborteaux. "What kids?"

The sheriff, Laborteaux, and Pollard whipped their heads around.

Kevin, Slade, Wendy, Rut, and their bikes were gone with only a branch swaying back and forth.

Laborteaux threw down the twig. "Dadburnit!"

"I'll get 'em!" Sheriff Traynor pulled his weapon and darted into the opening where the teens had emerged earlier.

Pollard walked briskly toward the sheriff's car and took the driver's seat.

Laborteaux pointed at Frank, Bill, and Jesse. "Y'all best just head outta here. We'll handle this." He worked his large frame into the passenger seat.

Pollard moved the car back and forth to turn it around and headed in the opposite direction of Bill's truck.

"Well, now what?" Jesse asked.

Bill and Frank looked at one another.

Frank shrugged.

Dickie and Larry broke through the thick brush.

Bill blurted out, "They went—"

Dickie held up a hand. "We heard everything. Listen, you get back to town. Get over to the Piggly Wiggly and get Poteet. We can trust him. Call the sheriff in Longview. Just in case they're buddies with Sheriff Traynor, tell them you also called the Texas Rangers."

"Why don't we just call the Texas Rangers?" Frank asked.

"No idea if they even have Rangers near here." Dickie moved his crossbow shoulder strap from one side to the other. He placed his hand on Larry's back. "You've done a good thing here, son. Now you go back to town with them and help."

Larry nodded. "What about my friends?"

Dickie smiled. "I'll take care of this. You trust me?"

Larry nodded.

Dickie turned and headed back through the thick brush.

"Hop in the back," Bill said to Larry.

Bill maneuvered his truck back and forth with less finesse than Pollard had done with the sheriff's car. Tree branches slapped the sides of the truck.

Jesse reached up and placed his hand on the roof to brace

himself. "Mighty nifty driving, Bill."

• ◉ •

SLADE LED THE other three through a rough trail with few stretches of straight riding.

"I don't think this is right," Rut yelled.

"Yeah, it is. I know exactly where I'm goin'," Slade yelled back. "Kevin! Why were Frank and Bill out here?"

Kevin shrugged although no one could see him, as he brought up the rear and they all rode with eyes straight ahead.

Splash!

The other three slammed on their brakes to avoid crashing into the creek as Slade had just done.

Wendy placed her hands on her hips. "Oh, great. Idiot! We're goin' in circles. Right back at the creek."

Kevin turned to see if anyone had followed. "Shhh! Look, this will work. They probably think we're headin' that way." He pointed in the direction of the highway. "Follow me!"

They carried their bikes across the creek and then walked them along the bank.

"An opening," Kevin said. "C'mon."

No trail existed, but they had enough clearing to move their bikes and make progress. The adrenaline pushed them.

"Where are we?" Rut asked.

Kevin stopped. "You know what? Notice how it feels like we're goin' uphill?"

Rut dropped his head and huffed. "Yeah. It's killin' me."

Wendy pointed. "Suicide Hill. I can see the rocks."

"I ain't ridin' down that," Rut said.

"Yeah, but maybe there's a way around it." Kevin lifted his shirt to wipe the sweat from his forehead. "At least we can get out of here and over to the highway."

"Hold it right there!" the sheriff yelled from fifty yards behind them.

"Oh, crap!" Rut yelled.

All four pushed their bikes at full speed toward Suicide Hill.

Laborteaux and Pollard had found the sheriff but could not drive any further down Devil's Backbone, as the road tapered off into a trail, and then there was no semblance of anything man-made.

The sheriff held up both hands, signaling for them to maintain their position. The pistol remained in his right hand. He heaved breaths through a drenched shirt and was far too out of shape to chase four teens through the Mead Creek woods. His determination gave him enough endurance to continue.

Laborteaux and Pollard's age prevented them from following the sheriff.

The teens reached Suicide Hill and stopped their bikes on the giant rock. It looked steeper and more dangerous with the reality of what faced them.

Wendy whipped her head at Kevin. "We ain't really doin' this, are we?"

"Oh, crap! Oh, crap! Oh, crap!" Rut cried. "Let's just tell him we don't know nothin'. He won't really hurt us."

Kevin's face turned red. "I think they found out Mrs. Oberlin was helpin' us. I bet they made her crash. Do ya think they'd chase us for nothin'? They're crazy! They'll probably do anythin' to protect Ephraim Pollard."

Crunch! Crunch! Crunch!

"I'm telling you kids to stop right now!" The sheriff leaned against a tree and huffed.

"Screw it! I'm goin'," Slade announced. "Y'all follow me." He mounted his bike and dove down, fully committed. He braked, released, and maneuvered around rocks and small plants. His effective counterbalancing kept him upright as he reached the bottom in under ten seconds as if he'd done it a dozen times.

Wendy followed, less gracefully, but made it safely.

Rut took the plunge next, had no graceful movements, and screamed the whole way. He looked up at Kevin. "C'mon, it's easy!"

Kevin's teeth chattered. He inched his front tire to the edge.

"I see you there! Don't move a muscle!" Sheriff Traynor waddled toward Kevin.

Kevin looked over the edge.

Wendy cupped her hands around her mouth. "C'mon, Kevin! You can do it!"

The sheriff stopped at the bottom edge of the rock, twenty feet away.

Kevin turned toward the sheriff.

"You ain't gonna tell nobody nothin'. Pollard's Raiders protects their own." The sheriff raised his revolver and cocked the hammer.

Kevin's eyes widened, and he pushed his bike off the edge.

Bang!

The arrow entered the front of the sheriff's right shoulder. The arrowhead exited through the back and stopped four inches out.

"Ahhh!" he cried, dropping the pistol, and falling to the ground.

The fired bullet—diverted by Dickie's arrow—had missed wildly over Kevin's head and fell harmlessly in the woods.

As Kevin reached the bottom of Suicide Hill, he yelled, "Ride!"

Kevin flew past them as the other three followed. They headed in the direction of the highway.

Dickie walked up to the sheriff. His shadow reached out twice his height.

"You shot me! What's wrong with you? I'll have you . . . I'll—"

Dickie picked up the pistol and stuck it in the back of his pants. He leaned over the edge of Suicide Hill and saw the four teens riding furiously.

"I'm gonna die," the sheriff cried.

Dickie shook his head. "No, you aren't going to die. If I wanted to kill you, you'd be dead right now. That arrow would be in your heart. What we have here is a clean through and through. You'll survive. Hurts like the dickens, though, I'll bet."

The sheriff looked up. "You don't know what you've done, you crazy old coot."

"I think I do." Dickie shouldered his crossbow. "I saved that innocent young boy's life. I think you know something about who killed my family. I think Laborteaux does as well, and you're both covering up for Ephraim Pollard. I plan to do something about it." Dickie looked left and right, then helped the sheriff to his feet. "I'm not having this discussion with you three out here, however. We'll get the proper authorities involved." He pointed in the opposite direction of Suicide Hill. "You walk that way, and you'll find your friends. Don't you think about coming to my place or after those kids." Dickie turned and disappeared into the woods.

Sheriff Traynor held his left hand over the wound—his fingers split around the arrow—and staggered toward his car.

───── • ❖ • ─────

TEXAS RANGER DELBERT Grove grew up listening to his grandfather, also a Texas Ranger, tell of his exploits in the Mexican Revolution. However, he spoke more about the Claymore murders than anything else from his career. Grove often found his grandfather studying photographs of the murder with his magnifying glass. He'd lift his head, look out the window to ponder, and return to the photo. His tales inspired the young Delbert to join the Rangers.

Although Delbert Grove had never investigated the murders himself, he knew the cold case better than most. When the Texas Rangers received a call from the *Dallas Times Herald* about a young librarian claiming new evidence, Grove and his partner chose to make the drive to Mead Creek.

News traveled fast in the small town, and it only took the Rangers two inquiries to find out that Kim Oberlin had been admitted to the hospital.

They entered her room and removed their hats. "Ma'am," Grove said with a nod. They both wore khaki pants, white button-down shirts, and brown ties. Each held a straw cowboy hat.

Her husband, David, stood and shook their hands. "Please, have a seat."

The hospital bed propped Kim up. She could barely see out of one eye and ached all over, but was otherwise alert and ready to talk. She proceeded to trade Claymore murder details with Grove and then added her and the teens' new discovery.

Kim grunted and shifted in the bed. "Sheriff Traynor got really dismissive. Ushered me out of his office. As I was leaving, well, that's when I noticed it."

"Noticed what?" Grove scooted to the edge of the bedside chair.

"The Pollard's Raiders emblem. Big and bold on a plaque in his office. It was on the wall opposite his desk, all alone on the wall. He had other plaques and things hanging on the others. But this one stood out. It was special." She pointed to a wall in her hospital room, imagining the scene. "I thought to myself, is he part of this? Keeping some secret? I've heard rumors of that just like anyone but never thought them to be true."

"And that's when you called us?" Ranger Grove asked.

"Yes, sir. Drove around the corner to the nearest pay phone

and called my friend at the *Dallas Times Herald*." She reached for her blackened eye. "It was him. After I left, I noticed the sheriff following me. Then he sped up and swerved in front of me. Forced me off the road and into a telephone pole."

"She just told me that part an hour ago," David said. "I didn't know who to call. There're two deputies, but . . . I'm not even sure if I trust my own pastor. You see, he's Ephraim Pollard's son. He's here in the hospital now. Went for coffee."

"Traynor, huh. Seems my granddaddy had some notes about a Willie Traynor. Wished he would've asked him more questions. Thought he might be the key to all this but never could quite put his finger on it. He still around?"

"That's the sheriff's father. You'll find him working at Pollard's Hardware," David said. "Ephraim might be there as well."

Grove leaned toward his partner. "Guess we better get some backup down here."

His partner nodded, stood, and exited the room.

The Ranger put his hand on top of Kim's. "You're safe now."

Pastor J. C. burst into the room with a cup of instant coffee from a vending machine. "My goodness, what's all this?"

David and Ranger Grove gave one another a cautious stare.

"You the pastor?" Grove asked.

"Yes, sir! Pastor J. C. Pollard. First Baptist Church of Mead Creek."

The Ranger stood, extending his six-foot-four frame. "How about you showing me where this Pollard's Hardware store is?"

CHAPTER 28

DING! DING! DING!

Ranger Grove entered the hardware store as the rusty bell alerted the staff. He removed his sunglasses and poked them into his front breast pocket.

His partner and the pastor followed behind.

Grove walked over and rested an elbow on the counter.

The beehive-haired cashier cocked her head. "Can I help ya?"

"You got an Ephraim Pollard around here?"

She leaned over the counter to see Willie Traynor kneeling at the end of an aisle and fingering through tiny drawers of various screws. "Willie, c'mere a minute."

Pastor J. C. stooped over and whispered to Ranger Grove. "He's worked here probably sixty years. Long-time friend of my daddy."

Traynor sheepishly approached and rubbed his hands on his pants. "Can I help ya?"

"Do you know where Ephraim Pollard is?"

"Why, no, sir. I—"

The Ranger slowly cocked his head and worked his sight across the Pollard's Raiders flag behind the register. He returned to Traynor. "Something tells me you know a little something about this flag."

Traynor looked at the flag. "Uh . . . well . . . that flag?" He pointed toward it.

Grove nodded.

"Yes, sir."

Grove turned toward the table. "How 'bout we have a seat and you enlighten me on it?"

They took their seats, Pastor J. C. joining them.

Grove's partner stood near the front door with eyes on the entire store.

Traynor had told the story of the flag hundreds of times with the enthusiasm of a tour guide. He presented a somber tone on this occasion.

"Sounds like you've known Ephraim a lot of years?" Grove asked.

Traynor looked at Pastor J. C.

"It's okay, Willie. Just answer the questions," Pastor J. C. said.

"Yes, sir. Since we was youngins."

Ranger Grove reached for a ballpoint pen lying on the table and began to spin it, repeatedly. He stared at the pen and avoided eye contact. "Mr. Traynor. What if I told you that I know a whole lot about the Claymore murders? For instance, I know that the victims were all killed with a shotgun. That three males were seen running away from the scene. That a shotgun has been found near the scene of the crime."

Traynor stared at the spinning pen.

Grove stopped it and looked up. "That it's got that Pollard's Raiders emblem on it."

Traynor rocked, rubbed his thighs, and then his face.

Ranger Grove grabbed Traynor's forearm. "You know what happened, don't you?"

Traynor nodded.

Pastor J. C. stared in silence.

Traynor nervously rearranged an ashtray and coaster on the table before looking at the Ranger. "Ephraim hated Mr. Claymore. With a passion. He was always fussin' that Claymore killed his daddy by sendin' him off to prison. Would keep sayin', 'one day he'll pay!' It was back in nineteen and twelve, after his granddaddy died, Ephraim got that shotgun that some Pollard's Raiders had given his granddaddy. He was showin' it off, showin' the emblem. Came and got me one Sunday after church and wanted to go down to Devil's Backbone and shoot it. We got Carlisle Laborteaux to go with us."

"You mean the politician?" Grove asked.

Traynor nodded. "We was all pretty young then. 'Bout fifteen I s'pose. We spent a lot of time out in those woods. We'd pretend to be fightin' the Battle of Mead Creek. I always got stuck bein' a darn Yankee. I hated that.

"That day, we rode out there, but I didn't have a horse, so I rode on the back of Ephraim's. We tied 'em up and went runnin' around out there shootin'. We were walkin' back toward our horses when Ephraim stopped. He was lookin' at the Claymore place. He turned red and was stewin' up hate. Carlisle said we should go scare 'em a bit. I knew that was trouble and argued against 'em, but I lost.

"We walked up to their place. Ephraim had the shotgun.

"He yelled out, 'Claymore! Get out here! We wanna talk to you!' He yelled like that a couple times.

"Finally, Mr. Claymore walked out in his Sunday best. They exchanged a few words with Ephraim makin' no sense and Mr. Claymore tryin' to calm him down.

"We were standin' about thirty yards from the porch. Mr. Claymore came off the porch and was tellin' Ephraim to calm down. Carlisle kept agitatin' Ephraim. Told 'em not to take no fluff off of Claymore. Ephraim told Carlisle to shut up and had his shotgun pointed at the ground, but Carlisle kept eggin' him on. I was standin' a few yards back.

"Mr. Claymore said, 'Boys. Calm down.'

"That's when it happened."

Traynor rubbed his thighs again and began with a broken voice, "Carlisle grabbed the barrel of the shotgun and lifted it toward Mr. Claymore, but Ephraim pulled back. Carlisle reached again and pulled the trigger. Mr. Claymore fell straight back. Blood just covered his chest.

"'What the hell did you do?' Ephraim said.

"Carlisle had this crazy look on his face. Just crazy! I was panickin'. I didn't know what to do. Then, we looked up and saw Mrs. Claymore in the doorway. She screamed and then ran back in the house.

"Carlisle ripped the shotgun from Ephraim's hand and ran toward the house after her. Ephraim followed him. I heard more screamin' and another gunshot. I was just frozen. I looked down at Mr. Claymore, and his eyes were still open. I finally tried to go yell at 'em to stop. I got to the porch and saw Mrs. Claymore lyin' face down at the other end of the house.

"Ephraim was standin' halfway up the stairs. He looked at me. He said, 'He's gone dadburn crazy,' ya know, referrin' to Carlisle.

"We heard another gunshot and Carlisle came runnin' down the stairs. I took off and they were right behind me.

"Carlisle yelled for us to stop. 'What about that Dickie?'

"'Forget about him,' Ephraim said. 'He's probably off in the woods.'

"Carlisle paused and looked over the property.

"Ephraim yelled, 'C'mon!'

"Ephraim might've saved Dickie's life by convincin' Carlisle to leave.

"We ran for our horses down near Meyer's Pond. That's when Carlisle had the idea to bury the shotgun. So, we buried it there by the creek. I was scared out of my mind. Even Ephraim was scared of Carlisle that day. He just went crazy. Said he'd kill us both if we ever told. Said we're Pollard's Raiders and we protect our own. Said killin' the Claymores was no different than killin' Yankee invaders in the Civil War." Traynor looked down and fiddled with the ashtray.

A crowd had gathered outside the hardware store. It didn't take long for news of visiting Texas Rangers to travel through town. Another pair of Rangers arrived and parked down the street.

Ranger Grove removed his hat and set it down on the table. He smoothed over his hair. "So, you're telling me it was Carlisle Laborteaux that fired all the shots?"

"Yes, sir. I mean, I didn't directly see the last two shots, but he had the shotgun the whole time after killin' Mr. Claymore.

"I think Ephraim would've confessed back then. It's been Carlisle this whole time that made us keep it a secret. I tried to tell this newspaper man once. Crowley, I think his name was. Somehow Carlisle found out and scared him off. Scared me too. From then on, I just keep pretendin' what was done was for Pollard's Raiders.

"I even got my son, the sheriff, all crazy about it. He's always sayin' we need to keep the Raiders alive. They're the real law in this town. Guess I've just been in some kind of denial. But there it is. Now I've confessed. I'm ready to face my crime."

"It all makes sense now," Pastor J. C. said. "My father has been coming to see me a lot lately. He never told me about the murders, but he kept saying he did something terrible once and was worried he was going to Hell for it. I just thought we were having pastor–congregant conversations. I'd ask him what this terrible thing was, but he wouldn't answer.

"My God!" The pastor covered his open mouth. "He said he told my mother on her deathbed. And his mother, my grandmother, knew. Said my grandmother knew from the beginning. Told him to always keep quiet about it." The pastor looked at the Ranger and shook his head. "I don't know what you must think of us, my family and this town. But that whole Pollard's Raiders mystique was important to them. And I always sensed that part of it was to keep some secret.

"It's like a secret society that only exists to keep one secret."

———————•●•———————

DICKIE DROVE UP and down the highway twice before he saw the four teens flagging him down. Kevin and Wendy sat up front, with Slade, Rut, and their bikes in the back. They stopped by Dairy Queen to find Larry as Bill gave them the news of the Texas Rangers already in town.

Dickie drove slowly down Main Street. He spotted Ephraim Pollard and Carlisle Laborteaux walking through the alley toward the front of the hardware store.

He parked in one of the slanted spots across from Pollard's Hardware. "Wait here," he said to the teens. He carried the shotgun. Its fractured wood and rusted barrel presented no threat to anyone.

Kevin and Wendy exited the cab and joined the other three in the back of Dickie's truck.

The crowd gathering near the hardware store had tripled.

One of Sheriff Traynor's deputies held up a hand for Dickie to stop. "Now, just where do ya think you're going?"

"I have an appointment with those Rangers," Dickie said.

"Arrest him!" Laborteaux yelled out. "That son of a bitch shot the sheriff. We just took him to the hospital."

The deputy looked at Laborteaux, confused.

"You hear me, boy? I said arrest him. Didn't you idiots get the call?"

"I don't think so," Ranger Grove said after stepping onto the sidewalk. He waved for the other Rangers to join him.

"You know who I am, boy?" Laborteaux said. "I'm the Honorable Carlisle Laborteaux, and I say what goes on in this town. You might have jurisdiction over this pissant deputy, but not over me."

Ranger Grove sniffed. "Laborteaux, huh?"

Laborteaux nodded, stuck his thumbs in his pants, and pulled them up. He quieted, sensing some respect from the Ranger.

Grove looked at the man standing next to Laborteaux. "Let me guess. Might you be one Ephraim Pollard?"

Pollard nodded.

"Arrest those two," Grove said to the other Rangers.

Pollard dropped his head and went silently.

Laborteaux cried out, "Do you realize the people I know? I'll have your star! I know the governor!" He continued with various pleas as a Ranger pushed his head down into the back of their car.

Grove approached Dickie. "Are you Mr. Claymore?"

"I am. And I guess you have some things to tell me," Dickie said.

The Ranger looked over toward the cafe. "Yes, sir, I do. How about I buy you a cup of coffee?"

Dickie nodded.

"You mind if my partner takes that old shotgun?" Grove asked.

Dickie handed it to the other Ranger. "Notice that special emblem on what's left of the stock."

Dickie and Ranger Grove walked across the street.

"My granddaddy told me a lot about you. He was a Ranger as well. You're a brave man, Mr. Claymore."

Dickie stopped him next to his truck. "Ranger, let me introduce you to the real brave ones. These are the five that solved this crime." Dickie choked up. "I owe them everything."

They each smiled in response.

Ranger Grove leaned on the truck. "So, you're the five rascals Kim Oberlin told me about?"

"Yes, sir!" Kevin said.

The Ranger removed his hat, wiped his brow, and returned it. "I never would've thought this would come down to some teenagers bringing down some old men."

———————— •◉• ————————

THE FIVE TEENS rode down Main Street and around the veterans memorial discussing their eventful day. They entered their neighborhood and stopped at Wendy and Rut's driveway.

"What do y'all wanna do tomorrow?" Rut asked.

Kevin shrugged.

"Let's go swimmin'," Slade said.

"Maybe after noon. Let's go to the fort first. Do some crawdad fishin'."

"Cool." Rut rolled his bike toward the garage.

"Come get us at ten," Wendy said.

"Cool," Kevin said.

Kevin, Larry, and Slade rode toward their street, side by side.

EPILOGUE

THE PROSECUTOR GAVE Willie Traynor a plea bargain for his testimony. He kept his job at the hardware store until his death in 1984.

Carlisle Laborteaux was sentenced to death but died in prison of natural causes before the sentence could be carried out.

Ephraim Pollard had no intention of facing his verdict. After posting bail, he stuck a shotgun in his mouth and pulled the trigger. The brand new shotgun had a Pollard's Raiders emblem on the stock.

Mayor "Stump" Pollard resigned. No one ever proved he had any knowledge of the crime, but he chose to retire in quiet with the Pollard name tarnished.

Sheriff Traynor spent ten years in prison for two counts of attempted murder. After his parole, he was last seen working in one of those oil quick-change places in a nearby town.

Pastor J. C. turned over the pulpit to David Oberlin. Kim Oberlin made a full recovery and became everyone's favorite teacher at the junior high.

Kevin Bishop, Slade Littlejohn, Larry Woodard, Wendy Rutledge, and Damon "Rut" Rutledge found their names in the papers for weeks after. Television news crews from major cities covered the story with one showing a short clip of an interview with Kevin and Slade.

The day after their 1985 high school graduation, Kevin and Larry decided to drive down Devil's Backbone and visit Dickie. They noticed him at the cemetery, sitting against a post as he often did. They parked and approached, but Dickie didn't turn and wave. He lay still. Eyes closed. He seemed at peace. A copy of *Tom Sawyer* was in his lap.

Kevin's plans for a deeper relationship with Wendy never materialized. Their high school years had reduced to casual glances and waves in the hall. She left Mead Creek for nursing school and never looked back. The last he'd heard, she had married and divorced, and now works at a hospital in a nearby state. Whenever he hears Boston's "More Than a Feeling," he thinks of her, and that day of sneaking through the Claymore mansion.

Rut joined the Army and served in Desert Storm. The military paid for his college, and he followed that with law school. He can be seen on the occasional billboard in Dallas, advertising for those experiencing a recent auto accident.

Larry still lives in Mead Creek, selling most residents their home and auto insurance.

Slade's hair went fast as did his slender abdomen. He found the Lord and is the most honest used-car salesman in an affluent Houston suburb.

Kevin teaches history at Mead Creek High School and night courses at the junior college in Cranville. Occasionally, a student will ask if he's the same one that solved the murders. The Claymore murders were his one and only attempt at detective work.

He and Larry are still close friends and love swapping the same childhood stories over and over. The Oz Arcade morphed into a video store and is now a coffee shop. Larry and Kevin meet there once a month or so to catch up.

The Claymore mansion sat empty for two years after Dickie died as attorneys litigated his will. Mead Creek residents gossiped that he had a ton of money stashed away somewhere. The truth was that he kept $18 million spread across six banks. The intent of his will won out with a portion going to Sheriff Brown's family in memory of the Browns caring for him after his family had been killed. The bulk went to several non-profit foster and orphan care groups. The five teens never knew it while Dickie was alive, but he had also set up $10,000 in savings bonds for each of them.

He left the mansion to the town's historical society. Through the years, developers converted Devil's Backbone to a four-lane road with housing developments on both sides. The historical society attempted to use the mansion as a bed and breakfast and spread rumors of hauntings to attract business. For many years, it was the most popular local destination on Halloween. Now it's a museum, and it has been restored to look exactly as it did in 1912. Most visitors say the secret passageway is worth the price of admission.

A small part of the woods around Meyer's Pond remains as it has always. In 2016, some young teenagers were playing there near the creek.

One of them jumped up and down on a pile of wood with large sections stacked one on top of the other. "Hey, check this out!"

"Cool!" his friend said. "We should use this to build a fort."

Cheryl Tiegs' pink bikini poster—weathered and faded—lay between two pieces.

Acknowledgements

NOVELS ARE RARELY written in a vacuum. This one certainly wasn't. Never have I asked so many people for little ideas and bounced nostalgic tidbits off them. This story reflects many of those bits of American life in the late 1970s, and I'm thankful for that group effort.

Thanks to my wife, Holly, and our five children, Kevin, Brandon, Jordan, Jadyn, and Megan, for their support as I pondered and wrote.

Thanks to David Nott for helping with ideas for cover art.

Thanks to the Rockwall Christian Writers Group for enduring first drafts and offering critiques.

Thanks to my beta readers: Nick Williamson, Regina Stone Matthews, Luke Krawietz, Leah Hinton, and Jennifer Johnson.

Thanks to my editor, Lauren Ruiz of Pure-Text.net, who is a genius!

Thank you, proofreaders: Mary Norsworthy, Debbie Vines, and Nancy Woodall.

I hope you enjoyed Summer of '79. Would you mind posting a review and telling a friend about the book?

Join the mailing list at *www.darrensapp.com* for writing news and release dates of future books. You will not be spammed.

Made in the USA
Middletown, DE
21 April 2018